Nine-Tail Trial

Written by: Serathin Sabertooth

Cover art by: Buckoviskiart

Published by Black Phoenix Productions

WARNING WARNING WARNING

This book is extremely adult in nature and therefore should not be read by minors. If you are considered a minor in your state or country or is uncomfortable with such material please do not read.

Contains the following:

- Sex between males
- Transformation
- Tentacles/Vines
- Muscle Growth
- Mind Control
- Plants
- Rubber/Latex

Table of Contents:

Chapter One – End of a Trial, Start of a Journey

Xavier stopped to take a rest on a tree trunk that sat next to the natural trail he had been hiking on, quickly opening his water bottle to take a drink as he let his breathing return to normal. Normally by this point he would already be back at his car but he had opted to try a new trail route that looked like he they had freshly marked and looked rather interesting to try out. It turned out to be much longer than he had expected but fortunately for the red and white furred fox he usually overprepared for his journeys anyway as he shifted the pack on his back. Better to have too much and not need it then need something and not have it, he thought to himself as he munched on some trail mix once he had recovered from the hike up the hill he had just undergone.

As the fox continued to hydrate and eat he mused that while it was a long trail it was also certainly a pretty one. The canopy overhead allowed for streams of sunlight to fall down on the path and he also saw the trickle of a stream that ran near the path. It was almost idyllic in a way and it made him wonder if the parks department actually planned it out instead of just doing what they usually did and cut out a new path whenever they needed more people to visit the area. It was hard to believe that anyone would put that much effort into something that only a few people like him would enjoy, but as the fox brought his pack around his shoulders once more he didn't question his good fortune and instead continued on the trail as it wound further up the hill.

About twenty minutes later Xavier looked down when he felt something hard underneath his shoes and when he looked underneath he found that the dirt had started to turn to stone. Even though it was worn away it looked like it was placed there deliberately, and as he continued to go further up he began to notice other stones that looked sculpted as though by the hands of a mason even if they were covered in vines. Perhaps someone had taken the effort to make this trail really nice, the fox thought to himself as he kept moving and found more overgrown artifacts that he passed by. Finally when he got near the top of the hill he walked through a heavily vine-covered archway that looked like it was some portal to another dimension, which prompted Xavier to stop and look around as he stood at the threshold.

Was this some sort of abandoned temple, Xavier asked himself mentally as he looked around the quiet area. He didn't see any signs that said he couldn't go in and it didn't even look like anyone had visited this place in a very long time. It was also the end of the trail, which caused him to groan since that meant that he would have to go back the way he came instead of go around in a loop like most of the paths in the park went. While he had left early enough that he would still get back before dark Xavier was hot and sweaty from the first leg of his journey and went inside to see if there was somewhere he could relax for a break, or see if the temple was possibly operational and someone could give him directions for a faster route.

As he walked through the gate and into the main courtyard Xavier saw a number of statues, all of them were vulpine in nature and most with multiple tails including the largest that stood on a pedestal over a leaf-covered pool of water that might have been a fountain. They were all kitsunes, and though the fox knew of the mythos that surrounded the mystical creatures he never thought that anyone ever worshipped them, especially not in his area. Whomever used to be here though had already cleared out a long time ago as he investigated the area to find that the buildings that remained intact were devoid of furniture and had thick, heavy layers of dust in them. Xavier opted to stay outside instead where the leaves overhead continued to keep the sun out and the heat at bay, flower petals and leaves swirled around his feet as he went over towards the water feature that ran through the middle to have his impromptu lunch.

Just as he set his pack down however Xavier noticed something that caught his attention; it was a small stream and waterfall that had been cut into the stone that led to the fountain pool before the water trickled down into the larger building opposite of the gate. He hadn't went that way to look and as he watched the liquid splash down from the man-made river he noticed that unlike the water in the pool itself this was so clean and clear that it looked good enough to drink. Fortunately he didn't have to risk drinking it as he had his own water supply, which he took a swing out of as he started to follow the path of the water into the nearby building. When he looked around inside he found that while the walls were covered with the same vines as the other buildings these particular stones had a number of flowers the fox had never seen before that were in bloom with petals that almost seemed to glow in the darkness.

The path of the water eventually led outside once more and Xavier could see the sun shine down on a pool of water that was surrounded by more stone mosaics of foxes with a singular nine-tailed kitsune statue that sat at the other end of it, all of it underneath an open-air roof supported by vine-covered columns. The fox's jaw dropped slightly in awe at the sight as the pool; not only at the artwork itself but also for the fact it was built on the edge of a cliff that jutted out from the cliff the temple was perched on and gave a spectacular view of the surrounding park below. Much like the water he had seen in the courtyard the pool sparkled with a clarity that allowed Xavier to see the large fox relief that was carved into the stone below. With the sun just in the right spot to make the surface sparkle he found himself tempted to take a little swim himself, though he shook his head when he reminded himself he was in a public park.

Although… since the trail didn't loop and seemed to end at this place he knew the only ones that could interrupt him would be those who would have had gone up the same trail as him. He hadn't seen anyone when he climbed up the hill and he could see a decent stretch of the path from this vantage point and saw the trail empty, which meant at the very least he would have anywhere from a few minutes to an hour in order to take a quick swim and refresh himself. Xavier found himself biting his lip as he considered his options but as the seconds passed the water continued to look increasingly tantalizing and finally he decided to throw caution to the wind and do it. Even as he went back to his pack to get the towel he stored there he couldn't believe he was about to do what he was thinking of doing, unaware that the flowers in the building had opened even more since he had first gotten there.

Since even he didn't think to pack a swimsuit with him, the plastic-wrapped towel he brough for getting caught in the rain or falling into a river, he knew if he didn't want to have to walk back with wet clothes he would have to go skinny-dipping. There was something thrilling about the idea though and as Xavier remained in the building to take off his clothes he found there was something freeing about being naked in the middle of the woods. Despite the risk that someone would see him completely naked he found himself keeping the towel in its wrapping instead of using it to cover himself as he walked back out towards the pool once more. The feel of the sun against his bare fur had him let out a slight sigh of contentment before he went over and lowered himself into the pool itself after a brief walk in the buff.

Xavier hadn't tested it ahead of time but found the sun-kissed waters were pleasantly cool without being too cold like most of the streams and lakes in the area. This was the first time that he had decided to do such a thing and the idea of being naked out here in the woods caused the smile on his muzzle to grow bigger as he brought his hands together to splash some of the water in his face. It was extremely refreshing and worth the potential exposure as he took the time to swim around in the pool. It wasn't too big but he managed to make a few mini-laps around while he let the liquid soak into him and revitalize his body, eventually putting his arms back against the side of the pool right next to the statue of the kitsune that looked over it.

"I hope this wasn't some sort of sacred pool, now that I think about it…" Xavier said as he looked up at the face of the statue and chuckled slightly. "Looks like you don't mind at all." As the fox continued to allow himself to relax he remembered the legends about kitsune and how they had to either be gifted those tails after an endurance of some sort of hardship, and when he counted them up and saw there were in fact nine it made him whistle. "Wonder what you had to do in order to get all those tails…"

"Would you like to find out?" A voice suddenly spoke up next to Xavier, the fox's eyes widening as he let out a cry and tried to jump back only to slide off the side of the pool and into the water. As he hovered there underneath the surface he looked up to see that there was someone who stood over it that managed to somehow sneak up on him, and as his mind raced on what to do since he was swimming in a public park completely naked eventually his lungs made the decision for him as he darted up to the surface and let out a sharp gasp when he broke through. "Sorry, didn't mean to startle you."

As Xavier caught his breath he continued to tread water about a foot away from the edge of the pool while he took a look at the one that knelt there. He was a fox like him, but unlike the red fur patterned with white on his chest, thighs, upper arms, and tail this vulpine was completely black-furred save for an iridescent green shine in the light. The mysterious stranger also had something that looked like black vines that coiled all over his body, and as he continued to swim there he noticed they shifted and moved a little like a snake. This creature isn't metahuman, Xavier's brain told him as the alien fox gave him a smile.

"W-who are you?" Xavier managed to ask once he had regained his composure.

"My name is Yavini," the fox said as he sat down and dipped his legs into the water, which caused the vines on his legs to start to slither out towards him and prompted Xavier to back away. "This used to be a temple that I had to abandon when a great fire swept through this area, though it appears most of the original stonework is still here and was merely reclaimed by the forests that grew up after it. I have to admit that I was surprised when I felt the presence of a creature in my pool and decided to take a look for myself.

With his eyes still on those vines Xavier couldn't believe what he was hearing, had this creature just said that he was the one who was worshipped in this place? "Are you saying that you were the one that they built this temple for?" Xavier asked, Yavini nodding in response. "But… you're not a kitsune, why all the artwork of them if you aren't one?"

"Because worship was not the point of his place," Yavini corrected. "Much like yourself back before the fires this entire area used to be the home for a number of fox clans, which was part of the reason why I had situated myself here in the first place, and for those who wanted to become my minion as well as a kitsune they would make the journey to this temple to… ascend. There used to be dozens of such creatures that made this place their home, sadly due to the fires and a stubborn nexus connection even the statues here are merely stone and only a little of my influence remains such as those flowers and this pool."

"So, you made kitsune here?" Xavier replied in shock as his mind tried to wrap his head around the idea while also trying to understand who and what this Yavini creature that sat before him was. "But… how?"

"As I mentioned before I can certainly show you," Yavini said with a grin on his face. "I'm actually looking for people that will roam the nexus realm while not under my direct control; in exchange for my power and a new look you'll still be loyal to me and help me out but you'll be outside my own realm. Of course if we go through with this and you decide you want to stick with me I wouldn't say no to that either, but at the moment we're looking for those who have the will and resolve to become nexus beasts."

Nexus beasts… realms… kitsune… even though the words swirled around in the head of the fox he wasn't quite sure how to string together the information that he was getting. It sounded like Yavini was making him some sort of offer, but other than becoming a kitsune he wasn't sure what it all meant to him. All he had wanted to do was take a swim in order to cool off for the hike back to the parking lot, but now he was in front of some sort of deific individual in their ancient temple and all while he continued to tread water while completely naked. What made him the most confused however was the fact that as soon as he saw that there was someone else that just appeared there next to him in this place that he hadn't just swam out and streaked naked all the way back down the hill while screaming.

After about a minute Xavier realized that he had just been floating there saying nothing and finally the other fox chuckled a bit and asked if he would like to come over and get a better explanation or if he would rather just enjoy his swim in private. Even as he realized he had been given a potential way out this dreamlike tale he still found himself intrigued enough by this Yavini to carry on with the conversation as he carefully swam over to the opposite side of the pool. As he was about to pull himself out of the water he stopped when he remembered he was naked, but when Xavier looked over at Yavini he saw that the self-described nexus creature was also nude. Eventually he just decided to go with it and sit on the side of the pool with his own legs in the water while he listened to the entire story.

Yavini seemed more than eager to fill in the gaps that made it hard for Xavier to understand the information he had been previously given, and as he went on about how he and his brothers had fantastical realms that indulged in the desires of those that aligned with theirs he eventually found himself shaking his head in complete disbelief. "But… I don't think I like plants that much," Xavier stated after Yavini told him that his sphere of influence was plants and flowers. "I enjoy hiking, but that's really about it I think."

"You'd be surprised how many people meet me like this and say the exact same thing," Yavini replied with a smirk. "However I think that not only are your desires more plant-based than you think, but you have to also realize that it's also about the type of creatures that I represent too that attracts me. Look at where you are after all."

Xavier found himself doing so and stared straight up at the large kitsune statue before looking back down at the plant fox. "I'm here because I wanted to subconsciously be a kitsune?" Xavier asked incredulously. "But the first time I even really thought about them was when I came to this place."

"This place would not have revealed itself to you if you didn't want to become one deep down," Yavini replied as he kicked his feet slowly around in the water. "I know you've heard the legends before, even if you don't remember it something about them created a spark in you that was big enough to cause the path here too be opened before you and lead you to this place. Of course I could be wrong too, it's been known to happen before, in which case all you have to do is leave this place and the knowledge of it and myself will evaporate from your mind by the time you make it back to your car."

The offer to simply let him go had blindsided Xavier and he found himself with a sudden existential crisis he didn't even realize he had. It only lasted for a few seconds, but when he saw the smug grin on the other vulpine's face he realized that this creature was right; somewhere in the recesses of his mind there was a desire to be a kitsune that he didn't even know he wanted, a feeling that was intensified when he felt a sense of panick by the possibility of this opportunity disappearing came up. "I suppose you might be on to something there," Xavier admitted as he felt himself blush slightly. "I've noticed more than once that I probably should be freaking out that some strange fox man covered in vines who claims to have been around when this ruined temple was new is offering me power and the ability to become a kitsune while I sit here naked."

"Couldn't have said it better myself," Yavini said as he stood up. "Also I'm not sure if you noticed the flowers in that building you went through but they release a mildly hypnotic pollen whenever they detect someone within, which when combined with my own natural charm makes sure that those who would be likely to deal with me quickly overlook my more supernatural aspects. Saves time in the long run, now come over here and let me get a better look at my potential new protégé."

Xavier found himself standing up even while he tried to process the fact that those flowers released hypnotic pollen, his fur dripping wet as he went over to stand in front of Yavini. He still felt awkward as he was stood naked in front of another man while he saw those vibrant green eyes look him over, realizing at this range that they didn't have a pupil and glowed with an unearthly light. Normally he wouldn't think about anyone getting his close, yet more than once he felt his body stay still with a mere shiver as the fingers of the other fox trailed down the red and white fur. More than once he was told to raise his hands or a leg up and Yavini inspected the thicker black fur on his hands and feet that traveled up to completely cover his forearms and shins before shifting to white as it got to his knees and ankles, then had him stand at attention while he ruffled the similarly colored mane that framed his collarbone and went down his chest.

"Not bad at all," Yavini complimented as he touched one of his longer finger claws before taking a step back. "Love the markings, will definitely keep those, and this extra fur around your arms and legs too for sure. I think you're going to make a lovely kitsune but before we start I want to give you one last chance to back out; if you tell me you want to be a kitsune with all the perks, power, and privileges that come with it then all you just have to say is yes, otherwise if you say no then you'll be free to head on back to your car with only the memory of a pleasant hike in your mind."

"I… um… can I think about it?" Xavier asked, which Yavini promptly replied with a shake of his head. It was clear that this was a once in a lifetime decision and somehow despite only knowing this creature for a few minutes he found himself nodding his head. "I want it, I want to become a kitsune, how do I start?"

“The journey of the kitsune is one that travels through not only my realm but also of those that I have great influence in,” Yavini stated as he slowly and dramatically waved a hand in front of the other fox’s face. “But before we can do any of that we have to make sure you are properly inducted, so first you must be reborn from the font of the kitsune and transported to the start of your journey.”

Before Xavier could ask what that meant the hand of the other vulpine that had passed in front of his muzzle suddenly grabbed him by the shoulder and pushed him back into the pool. The fox landed in the water with a loud splash and he sank nearly halfway down before he began to turn himself around to get back up to the surface. Before he start back up something wrapped around his ankle, and when he looked down to see what it was he was shocked to find that a thick plant vine had emerged from the mouth of the relief of the fox at the bottom of the pool and latched onto him! He tried to swim desperately up but several more emerged from different parts of the creature in the artwork and as he was brought down to the very bottom of the pool he looked up and saw that more vines had grown quickly across the surface of the water until it completely blocked out all the light from the sun.

There was a moment of panic that ran through Xavier and as he floated in the water he realized there was nowhere he could go in order to try and get oxygen, especially since the vines continued to make their way up his shins and coiled around his calves to anchor him in place. As the fox continued to look around however he suddenly saw one of the vines that had come up from the bottom of the pool float right in front of his muzzle and he found himself staring at it in question for a few seconds before it pushed forward. The texture of the plant was quite smooth and as soon as he felt it slide completely over his maw a hint of a sweet scent entered into his nostrils. He could feel it start to suction against the short fur of his muzzle and when he began to feel it press against his lips and snout he took a breath and found his lungs filling with fresh air.

Xavier's eyes widened in slight surprise as he took a couple more breaths and allowed himself to acclimate. His mind buzzed as the sweet, flowery scent continued to filled his nose and the highly oxygenated air filled his chest, and with his breathing needs completely met his floating there in the darkness actually felt rather serene. Within the confines of the plant muzzle a small smile began to form on his face as a strange sense of bliss filled him, one that caused his maleness to twitch as more vines slithered up and slowly wrapped around his cock before coiling around the throbbing shaft. The water made the slithering tendrils glide effortlessly on his flesh and caused him to let out a moan that was absorbed by the bulb that had enveloped his muzzle.

As the threat of being drowned subsided and the pleasant buzz that came from breathing in the sweet scent increased his floating in the water seemed to become more surreal in nature. With no light coming from the surface above it was hard to tell where he ended and the water began, but what did help was the vines that continued to spread over his body. With no way to see the vulpine was taken by surprise as a larger one began to push up underneath his tail, and as it did the vine that was on his muzzle began to push into it. The smaller tendrils swirled around his tongue and he could taste something sweet before it pushed to fill in his maw at the same time as the one at his tailhole spread open his rear and slide inside of him.

If it weren't for the thicker plants that were wrapped around his limbs keeping him in place Xavier would have bucked when the vine behind him finally spread him open. Whatever sap oozed out of the vines caused the inner walls of his tailhole to tingle just like his mouth did. Whatever the nexus creature was doing to him caused a surprising amount of pleasurable sensations to flood through his body. The arousal that he was getting as the vine seemed to hit every sensitive area inside him while he was being spread open and it seemed to cause his cock to get even harder, but as it throbbed in the cocoon of vines he realized without seeing it that it was actually getting bigger.

That wasn't the only thing either; as Xavier wiggled and writhed from the stimulation he was being fed he could feel his tongue starting to thicken slightly, his mouth twitching as well as his muscles began to swell too. While he had always had a fit, toned physique he could feel the vines that were on his muscles wove their way through his fur he could feel them swell with new growth. After a particularly large push from the widening tentacle in his backside he also felt his spine pop like he was stretching, only to keep in that position as his body grew a few inches taller. The fox couldn't believe this was happening, though that thought was kept to the back of his mind through the haze of pleasure that came from the vines tendrils tickling his toes and fingers.

As more minor changes happened to his body Xavier's focus once more returned to his cock, which had begun to get stroked more fervently in time with the tentacles in his mouth and tailhole. It was clear that they were about to bring him to orgasm, especially as the one between his legs continued to press against his prostate, and it didn't take long for the vulpine to spill his seed due to their ministrations. The fox was so blissed out that all he could do was ride the wave of his climax as he felt his body getting manipulated once more, this time his upper body being put upright while the vines on his arms slithered off. Even when he felt the connection between them break however he could still feel something coiled around them, though in the pitch darkness it was impossible to tell what it was as a similar sensation happened to his legs.

While Xavier was untangled from the vines that had kept him in the water the ones that had stretched over the surface of the pool also began to retract. The effects of the aphrodisiac that had been pumped into his system was quickly wearing off and when he found the vine in his maw had completely pulled out he once more found the need for oxygen as he swam to the surface. As he did his entire body felt very strange, but he didn't take the time to examine himself as he made his way to the edge of the pool while swimming upwards. When he finally got to it and broke the surface of the water his mouth opened wide in shock when he found it was not only night, the moon peeking over the horizon of the woods, but that he was definitely no longer in the park.

"Welcome to the first step in your journey," a familiar voice said as Xavier shook the water from his eyes and looked to see Yavini still sitting there. "Did you have fun with your metaphorical rebirth?"

"You could say that," Xavier said as he hoisted himself out of the water, his longer claws scratching against the stone as he saw his thicker arms in the light of the emerging moon. When he turned himself over once he was on dry land and got a look at himself he definitely was more muscular than before, though he retained a lithe form as his red fur had turned a dark green. True to what Yavini had said he could see the patterning had remained on his body and he still had the thicker fur on his arms and legs, though as he brushed his hands through the green tipped black fluff he saw something that caused him to pull his fingers back in surprise.

"A few new adornments to my new plant fox," Yavini stated as Xavier watched the small vines slither out from his fur only to retract back. "Soon to be my new plant kitsune. Take a few more seconds to get accustomed to your new body, but we have to be quick since your first trial is a bit time sensitive."

Xavier nodded and slowly stood up, feeling the vines on his feet wrap around his pads as he gave his new physique a flex. As he did he felt something wiggle in his mouth and for a moment thought that there was still a vine in it, only to have his tongue wiggle out into the air when he opened his maw. It was a bright green and slightly more tubular in nature, and when he wrapped his fingers around it he found that it was prehensile as well. It wasn't the only thing that had gained such a quality either as the fox looked down at the new vine cock that hung between his legs. His new appendage was nearly a foot long and with enough concentration he could will it to move around, shivering slightly in pleasure as the still sensitive flesh coiled around his wrist as it began to stiffen.

Yavini quickly brought his mind back to the present and told him there would be more than enough time to play with that later, the nexus creature guiding his new plant fox to a couple of houses that definitely weren't on the horizon before as the moon slowly began to rise up into the sky…

Chapter Two – Trial by Moonlight

The temple and surrounding forest that Xavier had gone into during the day had completely vanished, replaced with rolling hills that stretched out as far as the eye could see as he walked with Yavini through the small village. It was clear that they weren't alone as he saw several pairs of shining eyes stared out from nearby windows before they were quickly shuttered as they passed by. Though it was hard to see in the shadows of their houses those inside looked vaguely lupine in nature, which was a bit of a shock since Xavier thought that Yavini dealt mostly in foxes. Maybe the nexus creature was about to task him with turning them into foxes or something, though the fact that his own body had changed had still filled him with awe.

Even though his body still was vulpine in nature there were enough changes to it that made it feel alien to Xavier, especially the vines hidden within and his other new increased attributes. It made him wonder what else had possibly changed since the vines had completely covered his body during his transformation, but when he looked behind himself he didn't see any more of the plant appendages that had sprouted off of him or his tail. The added muscle and height was still enough to throw him off slightly and more than once he jumped when one of the plant tendrils slithered around his toes and fingers before sliding back. As he continued to try and control the ones that were nestled within his forearm and shin fur he suddenly felt a hand on his shoulder that got him to stop.

"I want to make sure that you're aware of the reality of the situation when we step inside," Yavini said as Xavier looked in front of him and suddenly found himself standing before a large hut at the end of the road. "These are essentially alien creatures to you, but thanks to your little transformation you have been imbued with enough of my nexus essence to understand any language you happen to come across. That being said the role of a nexus beast can sometimes be to go into hostile situations for us and defuse them so that we can either continue to operate or de-escalate something, understand?"

"I… I think so?" Xavier replied as he suddenly found a weight had formed in the pit of his stomach. "I feel a bit like I'm being thrown into the fire here."

"Trust me, it's the best way to learn when it comes to these situations," Yavini stated with a small smirk on his muzzle. "Just remember that you're here to gain that tail of yours and to help them out with whatever they might need while remembering who you represent. Trust the instincts that I've given you and you'll have another tail wagging behind you in no time."

For a brief second Xavier had forgotten the real reason why he had agreed to all this in the first place with the transformation and the sudden change of scenery, looking back at the singular green and black tail that wagged behind him. It was hard to imagine more appendages that would be there but when he did it caused him to shudder slightly in desire before he returned his mind to the present. He waited for Yavini's cue, but when it didn't come he just looked at the plant fox in question. The nexus creature was quick to remind him that this was his trial and that he was merely there as a form of passive guidance and to transport him to the next location once he was done.

Xavier could feel a lump form in his throat when he found himself about to go into a strange house alone, and decided to knock first to keep from barging in unannounced. When he turned his head back towards Yavini he found that the nexus fox was gone, which caused him to gasp slightly in surprise. At that moment he realized he was alone the door opened and caused him to jump even more as he saw a large wolf man look out and ask what he wanted. The figure was rather imposing and at his original height Xavier might have had to tilt his head up to make eye contact, instead they were eye to eye as he thought of what to say before asking if they had a problem he could solve for them.

There was a brief scowl on the face of the man before he stepped aside and motioned for Xavier to step inside, which he promptly did. Inside of the large building it looked to be more a meeting hall than a domicile but the only ones there were an elderly wolf man and a somewhat skinny young wolf man that sat in front of a fireplace. “Elder,” the wolf at the door said, prompting both lupine heads to turn and look a them. “This one says that he can help us with our problem.”

“Well, I didn’t say that I could solve-“ Xavier started to say before he was suddenly brought forward by the other man until the two stood in front of the Elder wolf and the smaller one. “Oh, hello.”

“A fox,” the Elder stated as he looked up at Xavier with milky white eyes. “It’s been a while since anyone of your tribe has come to visit, and with such an unusual aura to boot. I suppose if anyone is going to solve our problem it could be you.”

“I still say that if you let me take the hunters out we will end this problem in one night,” the big wolf behind Xavier said with a slight growl.

“If this creature is as fierce and fearsome as those who had seen it say then I will not risk the slaughter of our hunters until we better understand what it is,” the Elder said, which prompted a huff from the bigger man. “Tell me fox, what is your name?”

Xavier quickly introduced himself, the Elder stating that it was fine to be called as such and told him the skinny wolf was Aegis while the bigger one was Dom. It was a very apt name for the latter, the fox thought to himself as he looked the muscular creature up and down, but quickly cleared such thoughts from his head to focus on the problem at hand. “For the last year now the village has been plagued by the presence of a creature that is not of this world,” the Elder said with a slight sigh. “A beast that looks like us but has the presence of a true predator, a hulking monster that only comes out when the moon is full.”

"When the moon is full…" Xavier repeated as he tilted his head in question. "Like a werewolf?"

"I… do not understand such a term," the Elder replied. "But the howls this creature produces echo through the valley and those who had dared to venture out into the night before had started to see more of its presence in the moors. It stands to reason that this creature is starting to become bolder, whatever has kept him away from this settlement is becoming less effective by the month and soon he may decide to attack this place."

Hunt a werewolf, that was something Xavier definitely didn't expect when he sighed up to try and become a kitsune. He thought that given the temple motif he would be meditating or searching for enlightenment or something, not trying to seek out something that could rip him to pieces. As he thought about it though Yavini didn't strike him as the type to send him on some sort of suicide mission, which meant there must be something else to it that utilizes the power of the plant fox. Since there was no way for him to go back home anyway, unless he wanted to give up on the quest he had just started and shout for the nexus creature to take him home, Xavier nodded his head and told the elder he would go and look into the problem.

"You can't seriously be sending him out and keep me here," Dom said angrily as the elder gave Xavier a nod. "I don't even need the other hunters, just let me go and find whatever is responsible for this and I'll bring back the pelt of the creature before dawn."

"I need everyone here in their positions so we can keep our forces centralized in case it decides to attack," the Elder replied. "So far the creature hasn't tried to attack anyone yet and if it is some sort of peaceful being or spirit then we may provoke its wrath. Plus I want to be sure all fighting forces are contained here to protect the settlement in case our new friend here fails, and of course Aegis I want you in your room as usual to make sure you don't get in the way of our hunters or Xavier."

Xavier could see the look of mirth in the eyes of the smaller wolf but Aegis didn't dare say anything, instead just give a small affirmation before he got up and went to a set of rooms on the other side of the hut. The fox watched him leave until the Elder turned to him and told him the general location where the sightings happened, as well as the time that the howls seemed to happen. When Xavier looked out the window he saw that it was already starting to get close to that time, so he thanked the two for the information and started out of the hut. For a brief second it looked like Dom was going to block his path but after the Elder cleared his throat the warrior wolf man gave him a look and stepped aside.

A minute later Xavier was back out into the night air of this new place and looked down in the direction that the Elder had told him. It looked like it was a marshland that was near the edge of the shore as the fox spotted the sparce trees that obscured the area. While it wasn't the forest that he had been hiking through earlier in the day, or had it been multiple days he wondered, it was the most likely an area that a beast of their description would hide from others. Even though it looked like it was near the settlement he knew that the hills made distance deceptive and he immediately started to make his way towards the location with the light of the full moon as his guide.

It took Xavier an hour to finally reach the edge of the wetlands and when he did he still had no idea what he was going to do when it came time to meet this creature. If it was some sort of werewolf he had little idea on what a plant fox could do to stop it, unless perhaps he had some sort of power that could pacify it he didn't know about yet. He also didn't get the connection when it came to the settlement above, if it's the werewolf he was supposed to be helping somehow than why not have Yavini start him there and just get the encounter over with? Something inside him said that such a thing wouldn't be that straightforward as he looked about for the most solid path through the marsh to began to trek forward.

"I wouldn't go that way if I was you," a voice called out that nearly made Xavier fall into the nearby water when he jumped, then turned to see Aegis looking at him from the top of a toppled over tree. "That area looks solid enough but once you get deeper in there's nothing but delta rivers that you have to trudge through to get back on dry land."

"What are you doing out here Aegis?" Xavier replied as he carefully made his way back. "I thought your dad told you to stay in your room."

"Huh? Oh, the Elder isn't my dad," Aegis explained as he reached out to help Xavier get back onto solid footing once more. "None of the wolves in the settlement are related, we're all just the hunters chosen to go to the settlement in order to take advantage of the summer migration. I'm supposed to be going with them but between my lack of… ability and this new monster popping up I've been stuck with tending to the elder hunter."

"Sounds rough," Xavier said as he followed Aegis down a different path through the swamp. "Is that why you snuck out tonight, going to try and help me take down the big bad wolf so that you can prove you're a hunter?" Aegis shook his head at that but remained quiet afterwards, and from the fact that he had a bow slung around his bare back and a knife connected to the leather loincloth he wore the fox believed he intended to do much more than just talk to this creature. Even though Xavier thought to press the matter he wanted to wait until they were a little further into the swamp since the wolf seemed to know where he was going at least and it would make his trip a little easier.

"Seems you know where you're going," Xavier commented as they passed underneath a set of fallen trees to avoid a large pool of water. "This isn't the first time you've snuck out to find this creature, is it?"

There was a moment of pause as the two stood there in the darkness of the tree's shadows as Aegis looked down. "With the Elder not needing me much I don't really have much to do so I sleep during the day and sneak out at night," Aegis admitted. "I heard that prey animals that wander into the swamp are easier to catch so I've been trying to give myself the advantage, and when I heard that the creature was in these parts it only made sense for me to try and hunt it too."

"Hunting a beast that even the Elder doesn't want the hunters to go after," Xavier said as they pressed forward. "Not sure if that's brave or foolhardy, one day you could just not come back and they would find your body floating in one of these shallows. That being said, it's a bit of a surprise that you've been out here every night looking and haven't found this creature yet."

"Other than the full moon he doesn't seem to make an appearance," Aegis replied. "I've found tracks of him though, as well as some tufts of fur here and there, but strangely he doesn't ever seem to leave the swamp and I've never been able to track his home. Maybe with you here I can finally start making some headway on this."

While Xavier admired the wolf's determination he wasn't sure if having him around was going to help at all. As the minutes turned to hours and the moon rose high up overhead the two didn't see anything that resembled a hulking beast and it had already passed the time that the Elder said the howling usually happened. Had his presence somehow spooked the creature, the fox thought to himself as they crossed several sunken logs to hop onto dry land in the middle of the marsh. As they pushed out into a set of thick shrubs that bordered the tree line Xavier was at least thankful that Aegis had tagged along, the wolf seemed to know where he was going as they broke through into the moonlit meadow.

Xavier was surprised at what they had found on the other side; dozens of pearlescent blue flowers were in full bloom underneath the light of the moon as they walked around the edge of the impromptu grove. The petals seemed to glow in the light and as they got closer the plant fox sensed a power there that caused his nose to twitch. Perhaps this was something that Yavini wanted him to find, he mused as he went over and knelt down next to one of the flowers that was still closed. At first he wondered why the ones closest to them weren't open like the rest but he quickly got his answer as the moon shifted its light overhead and caused the flora to unfurl and bloom in the light.

"These are quite the flowers," Xavier commented as he cradled the petals, and as he watched a small cloud of silvery pollen rose up in the air from the others that were open as well a chord of realization struck him. "Flowers that bloom in the light of the moon… Aegis, you've come across the grove before, right?" When there was no response the fox looked over at his lupine companion, who stood there and just stared at the flowers. "Aegis?"

"I… I know these flowers…" Aegis said as he stepped forward towards the flowers and Xavier, and when the wolf stepped in the moonlight the fox saw his pupils were completely dilated. "Yes… I've been here… I just… I need…"

Before Xavier could stop him Aegis darted forward and buried his muzzle into the middle of the flowers before inhaling deeply, wisps of silver pollen dust floating into the air while the rest stuck onto the wolf's muzzle. Almost immediately after the lupine creature let out a loud moan and fell to his hands and knees, but as Xavier got up to help he saw that the wolf had just put his head into another flower and continued to breathe in heavily. The fox just stood there and watched the wolf continue to go to each flower within reach the huffs and grunts that came from Aegis started to get deeper while his loincloth began to tent out. The leather loincloth quickly strained as Aegis tried to stretch to another flower only to have his neck pop and swell, which seemed to cause the transforming creature to back away and try to shake the silver off his growing muzzle as his teeth stretched out past his lips.

There was a loud ripping noise that brought Xavier's attention back to the wolf's groin as the quickly growing hips popped the belt off of him, causing his throbbing cock to flop out onto the ground as he flopped over onto his back. The shock that was on the face of the wolf quickly became tinted with pleasure as the skinny creature's frame started to bloat with muscle, his arms beefing up to the point where they looked almost comical on his still someone small body before the cascade of strength filled out his forearms. Aegis began to drool as his large claws furrowed into the ground while his chest went from flat to ripped in minutes, his fur growing thicker over his body still could only hardly hid the mountainous pectorals and washboard abs that were forming on the otherwise tiny stomach. Even though the pollen had affected his groin first when the swelling of muscle made it to his hips his cock went from diminutive to huge at that point as the stiff red flesh ballooned out until it was almost thicker than his legs.

As the beast that Aegis was becoming let out a deep howl of pure pleasure Xavier realized he had found his culprit; the wolf must have stumbled upon the patch during one of his night hunts and the euphoria that clearly came from his transformation had caused him to come back time and time again. Or it could have been the fact that as his bones popped to handle the massive amount of muscle to the point even his tail lengthened that he just liked being in this hulking form, especially since he looked much bigger than even Dom at this point. Either way as his member began to dribble silver cum and his feet swelled into massive paws the fox could consider the case closed, though as the eyes of the wolf opened and he could see they were silvered orbs he realized he had another potential problem on his hand.

When the new Aegis finished his transformation he immediately began to stroke on his new cock, and though Xavier could have left at that point he found himself rooted to the spot. His nose also itched slightly and when he reached up to scratch it he felt something hard on his muzzle instead of fur as he ran his claws against it. The fox was shocked to find it was one of his teeth that had poked past his lips and he looked down at himself to see that his body was growing too, though definitely not at the same pace as the wolf in front of him. The flower had released pollen into the air that he inhaled, the vulpine realized as his fingers and toes began to thicken, but instead of leaving to try and avoid the effects he found himself drawn to the flowers and the creature they had created. He found himself licking his lips as his thoughts became laser focused on the muscular wolf that drooled and growled as he pleasured himself, though as soon as Aegis once more sensed the other addled creature in the area he stopped and looked at him.

I shouldn't be doing this, Xavier thought to himself as his own cock began to stiffen, but as his instincts told him otherwise he started to figure this was possibly what Yavini had been talking out. If Aegis was in fact the one he was supposed to be helping than there was a reason he was out here with him, though it was becoming hard to think as the blood in his skull went somewhere else while his neck thickened and his shoulders became broader. "So you… you're the creature," Xavier managed to say the werewolf got to his feet, silver drool dripping from his toothy maw. "Why didn't you tell me?"

"Don't remember until now," Aegis replied, his voice much deeper than before as he closed the gap between the two. "The flowers always affect me, but the full moon turns me to this. Once a month I feel like an apex predator, not a weakling like the others see me."

"That you are," Xavier said as he began to run his hands up the thick muscles of the wolf's chest, his fur even thicker and softer than before they started to play down towards his thick tool. "Why not go back to the camp like this? Show them that you're the alpha."

Aegis looked at him with slight confusion, and with Xavier starting to lose track of the conversation himself from his growing lusts he imagined the wolf was even further gone. "I don't know what this alpha is you speak of, but I know that soon the pollen will turn me into a true beast," Aegis said with a growl. "I still have enough sense to not go to the settlement though, not like this, especially when the lust takes hold and my only thoughts are to hunt and rut. It's been getting harder though, I've been taking in more with each trip and each time I lose more of my former self."

"But… is that really a bad thing?" Xavier replied without even realizing it, causing the ears of the wolf to perk up as the fox realized he was onto something. "You want to be stronger than anyone, to find your place in the hunters, why not have it be as their leader? This inner beast has been in you the entire time, let the pollen unlock it so you have your true form..."

The werewolf let out a deep growl and Xavier could tell he was pushing a few buttons inside of him, though the fox wasn't sure how he was doing it. The words just seemed like the right thing to say and with the pollen also dulling his thoughts the idea of this creature dominating the others got his own vine cock as hard as a rock. For a few seconds the two remained still in that moonlit field and he could tell that with what little processing power he had left in his mind that Aegis was deciding whether to embrace the flowers or to hide and pleasure himself while worried about the other hunters as he usually did. The two could feel one another's cocks throb between them as eventually Xavier felt a large clawed hand come up against the back of his head and bring him in for a deep kiss.

A deep growl reverberated between the furred chests of the two of them as Xavier suddenly felt a large tongue press past his own lips, and as he used his longer one to reciprocate he felt his teeth and muzzle growing even more primal in nature. It appeared the pollen was retained in the saliva of the wolf and had caused his werefox transformation to progress more, though he didn't have much time to consider it as he felt himself get pushed into the field of flowers. A thick plume of silver pollen rose into the air as Aegis attempted to pounce on him, only for Xavier to roll away with a growl. As the silvered eyes of the creatures locked onto one another the fox felt his body start to grow again, though all his mind could think of was laying out that wolf and thrusting his cock deep inside of him.

The two wrestled with one another as both their physiques continued to swell, becoming even bigger as one tried to pin the other down in a show of dominance. Both smirked and licked at one another as they rolled around, feeling their thick fur and hard muscle press against one another as they enjoyed every second of it. With Aegis further along in his transformation though he managed to get the best of the plant fox even as vines tried to wrap around his massive limbs, and the fox eventually felt himself get pressed down with the heavy body of the wolf on his back. By this point both of them were nearing the eight-foot mark and they were much bigger than Dom was, but as Aegis took his foot-long cock and pushed it into the meaty cheeks of Xavier's tailhole it wasn't enough as he grabbed another flower and breathed in deeply.

Just how big did Aegis want to be, Xavier thought while he felt the other male growing bigger on top of him as his tailhole was suddenly stretched open. The fox's eyes went wide as the huge werewolf pushed deep into him with his first thrust, but after the initial shock he found that there was nothing but pleasure as his tailhole formed easily around it. It was likely another modification that Yavini had given him and he was thankful for it as instinct quickly took over Aegis and he quickly filled him with that throbbing shaft. As the fox squirmed in pleasure he could feel the wolf growing even bigger while inside him and as the silvery cum dribbled into his stomach it was causing his body to grow once more as well.

It appeared that Aegis wanted his impromptu partner that gave him such freedom the ability to experience the same and Xavier suddenly found a flower in front of his face while being rutted into. His already silvered eyes went wide as the pollen hit his system and gave him a heady euphoria while his muscles thickened even more. His claws dug deep furrows into the earth as the silver dust that covered both their bodies began to create an aura around them while the six-pack that Xavier had grown turned to eight, then ten as he was pulled back so the fox was on his knees. Both let out a deep, raspy growl as their feet shifted and grew into a new configuration, one that made them both look even more like beast men as Aegis continued to go hilt deep into the fox.

Xavier looked down and saw his muscular stomach bulge out each time the huge cock pushed into him completely while his heavy hands went down and stroked his own throbbing member. As the two werecreature muscle beasts had sex their act had inadvertently caused the destruction of a number of the flowers in the grove. It also seemed their own growth had peaked, both men drooling what looked like pure molten silver from their jagged teeth-filled maws as well as their cocks that splattered onto the ground. When the fox looked down at the torn up earth he could see something sprout up from the loose dirt, something that caused a grin to form on his muzzle as he looked back at the werewolf rutting him…

As the moon continued to drift through the night sky towards the other side of the horizon Xavier decided to bring the origin of the beast and the source of the roars to the Elder, after the two had had their fun with one another. Once more the plant fox found eyes on him again, but this time it was because he was a huge werebeast that strode next to a similarly-muscled wolf creature that made their way confidently down towards the main hut. As they did the cum and drool they dripped had started to grow more of the flowers in their wake, ones that by the next full moon would release more of the silver pollen in the air. They wouldn't be needed though; Aegis had become so imbued with their essence that he produced the pollen himself, his fur a permanent shiny silver as he leaned forward to knock on the door so that his erect cock didn't bump into it first.

Just as the door opened Xavier suddenly found himself no longer standing beside Aegis, instead he was on a hill that overlooked the settlement as Yavini stood next to him instead. "I figured that you had done enough to help our fine friend down there," Yavini said as Xavier watched Dom open the door and attempt to attack Aegis, only to be pushed back inside before entering himself. "Aegis thought that his need to be transformed by my Moonbloom flowers was a weakness of will, when actually it would give him the strength he needed to finally be accepted into his tribe."

"I sort of guessed those flowers were… whoa…" Xavier trailed off as he began to feel his body deflate, everything quickly returning to normal and the silver pollen that he had trailed into the wolf settlement dissolving from his fur. "That was… strange."

“The effects on you were going to wear off far faster than the others,” Yavini explained as the two continued to watch as others began to leave their huts, sniffing the air as the muscles on their bodies twitched slightly and began to grow. “Soon the Moonbloom pollen that Aegis is seeded with will spread over the settlement and create an entire group of hunter werewolves, which they will then likely continue to bring back to their main clan with them. Their transformations will be the greatest during the full moon, but for Aegis he is permanently in his current form and when the light of the full moon hits him he will spread that pollen and those flowers wherever he steps.”

Xavier looked on in awe as the heavily muscled silver-furred wolf left the hut a short while later, and when another large wolf man left after him the fox first thought it was Dom only to see the milky eyes before the silver completely enveloped them. “So he’s going to spread and change anyone he touches,” Xavier stated, to which Yavini nodded. “That’s why I was brought there?”

“You were brought there to help someone realize their true destiny,” Yavini replied with a small smirk. “For which you have already been compensated. Now we must move on, as much as I’m sure you’d like to join them we have much to do that could use the touch of a kitsune like yourself.”

As Yavini opened a portal between this realm and another Xavier looked at him in confusion until he looked back and saw that his green tail had been joined by another. The silver-furred wolf tail glinted in the moonlight as the two wiggled against one another in the air as the fox touched it in awe. He hadn’t even realized he had grown it with his other transformation happening and it looked as though he was an actual kitsune now. But that was only two tails… there were still seven to go as he was ushered into the portal to the next trial that awaited him.

Chapter Three – Trial of the Shadows

The portal Yavini had created once more took them to a land that was shrouded in night, but this time instead of rolling hills they were surrounded by huge trees that glowed with bright flowers on them. Xavier was still recovering from his time as a werefox and was glad that it didn't seem like anyone was there to immediately tell him what to do next. As he looked around though he found that there was no one around him, not even Yavini as a slight frown crossed his muzzle. It appeared that he would once more be left in the dark on what he was supposed to do, and this time there was no one that seemed to be around as he began to move forward.

As the two-tailed kitsune investigated the alien landscape he took a moment to check on his tail once more. It didn't feel like it was real, but every time he grabbed the silver fur he could feel it tug against his tailbone before he let it go. There was also something else that seemed to come with it, a sense of power that wasn't there before. When he attempted to try and figure out what it was it felt like his brain was blocked, a feeling similar to knowing a piece of information but having it be on the tip of the tongue without actually remembering it.

Eventually Xavier gave up on it and focused on the task at hand; Yavini had given him no clues this time on what he was supposed to do when it came to this place and the presence of the glowing flowers told him little. As he walked forward he looked down and saw that he left bioluminescent footprints in the moss and wondered if the nexus creature had a hand in this realm like he did with the Moonbloom flowers from the last one. Since this was another alien world though it was hard to tell anything and all he could do was continue to walk to try and find what he needed to do in order to gain his next tail. One thing that he could say though was the scenery was very pretty as he went over to some of the glowing orange and yellow leaves and brushed his hand against them to watch them light up in response.

Xavier was unsure of how long had passed during his wanderings until he came across a small pond that had tiny little seedlings that surrounded it. Unlike the others that he had seen so far these appeared to be in orderly rows, like someone had cultivated them to grow in that manner and made sure not to disturb them. When he circled the pond to see if there was anyone there or any buildings that would indicate a domicile he found nothing but what looked like a house that had become nothing more than a pile of rotten wood. It looked like no one had lived in this area for a very long time and as the kitsune got back to where he had started he found himself scratching his head in confusion.

When he looked down and saw his own footprints that went around the pond his eyes widened when he saw a second pair that was there which he knew he didn't make. The kitsune quickly looked around and wondered if someone was sneaking around trying to remained unnoticed, but when he went forward to examine them he saw they just suddenly ended a few feet away. He looked at them in confusion and then glanced around to see if he could find who made them, but no one was seen and the area was eerily quiet. When it was clear that he was alone, or at least made to feel that way, he carefully leaned forward and moved his clawed hand over the area where the footprints were.

While he didn't feel anything with his moment Xavier jumped back slightly when the footprints started to move again, this time it moved over towards the seedlings that he had seen before. The little plants were no more than an inch or so tall and seemed to be similar in nature to the ones that grew over the trees and on the ground where he had come in. In fact as he thought about it this appeared to be the only place that it didn't have such lush alien foliage and as he stood there he began to see something appear over the tops of the small plants. At first it was hard to tell but as the ghostly image got more opaque it looked like a set of three webbed fingers that briefly hovered over the plants, which seemed to respond by quivering slightly before they all stopped.

When Xavier examined the footprints that the ethereal creature created they also appeared to be webbed in nature, which made him believe that this one was some sort of aquatic species. With this new information the kitsune looked around and noticed that he could start to see others that flitted in and out of sight, like ghosts that only appeared when they were close to the glowing plants. Or perhaps that was how this particular species operated, that the flowers gave them enough strength to manifest and that the only reason they hadn't up until that point was because there was some strange creature stomping around. But that made the kitsune wonder even more why he was here, what sort of help he could possibly give these people that don't seem to be able to even communicate with him.

Once more Xavier's eyes went back to the seedlings that were around the pond and noticed they went into the water as well. The footprints hadn't left that spot and unlike the others that were starting to show themselves this particular one didn't seem to be able to manifest like them. Perhaps he was supposed to make the plants grow, he mused as he reached down to the soft earth and pushed his fingers into it. He let the vines that were nestled within his fur start to push over and he attempted to put the power of the nexus creature into it to stimulate the growth, only for the first one he touched to start to shrivel immediately.

There was a gust of wind and Xavier quickly pulled his hand back when he saw an outline of the creature appear about a foot on the other side of him, a shiver going down his spine as he figured this ephemeral creature had just passed through him to signal for him to stop. When he looked down at his own chest he was surprised to find that his white fur had turned a neon blue for a brief second before it faded back to its normal coloration once more. When the entity passed through him it was like a static discharge, and for a brief moment they were together he could almost sense what it was thinking. As Xavier looked back at the flowers the entity had impressed upon him that only their energy could grow their own flowers, but that he couldn't harness enough in order to allow him to manifest like the others.

The entire encounter was enough information for Xavier to get an idea on how to help this creature and as he turned to where the footprints stood once more he offered out his hand to it. After a few seconds where there was no response the kitsune frowned and thought about how to try and communicate with this creature on his potential plan. The fact that Yavini gave him the ability to comprehend all languages didn't help when they didn't speak, but as he looked down at the glowing moss between them he got an idea. He wrote down a few words by dragging his fingers in the moss to form letters, and after a few seconds he got a response that the creature's name was Nautlin.

With a line of communication established Xavier explained what he wanted to do and the creature responded by drawing a smiling face, which prompted the kitsune to hold out his hand yet again. This time it only took about a second before he felt something push into it, the black fur turning to a dark ocean blue as his skin began to stretch out between his fingers. The contact between them was electrifying but in a pleasant way, like a buzz from a massage chair as the coloration began to spread up to his wrist. As he began to feel his fingers twitch slightly he suddenly felt his hand droop down and the transformation quickly receded, which prompted Xavier to lean down and put a question mark between them.

Nautlin responded he didn't know and they tried again with the kitsune's foot, only for them to get his entire paw changed before Xavier felt his leg shift back. It was like his body was rejecting the energy, or that after it got to a certain point it forced him back. If this was going to work he needed to find a way to keep still, and when he relayed his thoughts to the other creature he suddenly saw an arrow point back towards what remained of the house he had first seen. It was strange for Xavier to see the footprints continue to walk beside him but at least he knew what it was now, and when they got to the wreckage the creature drew a picture of the kitsune moving the rubble away from a certain place.

While Xavier wasn't sure what he would find when he pulled the debris aside he was still surprised when he cleared off everything and found a lattice of vines on the other side. As he stood there a few feet away he could see the plants that grew along the metal start to move towards him, the tips wiggling in the air. It reminded the kitsune of the vines that he had encountered in the pool and it made him wonder if Yavini had his hand in the evolution of these people. When he waved his hands in the air and watched the vines continue to track his movement he saw something glow on the ground and saw that the ethereal creature had drawn an arrow towards the metal lattice.

"Yeah yeah," Xavier said as he took a deep breath. "I think I have an idea of what you want me to do now. This is definitely going to be an experience…"

After taking a moment to prep himself Xavier decided to put his back against it so that his muzzle wouldn't be squished against the lattice. He could already see the vines stretch even more towards him and the kitsune found himself shivering slightly as he turned around and slowly backed up into the apparatus. It only took a few steps before he could feel them start to press up against his back and shoulders and it caused him to shudder slightly when the bigger ones coiled up against his biceps. They were quite gentle but also very strong and by the time his fur pressed against the metal of the lattice the vines had slithered over his upper arms and thighs and managed to lift him up off of the ground.

Xavier let out a huff as the vines teased over his chest and made their way along their inner legs to form into a plant harness that rendered him increasingly immobile. He felt his own vines that were nestled in the thicker fur of his forearms and shins aided in his binding and looped around the metal to pin his limbs in place. The kitsune let out a huff as his arousal built, though the vines didn't seem to be actively attempting to stimulate him and instead seemed more focused on keeping him restrained. With his feet dangling a few inches above the ground there was nothing that

Xavier could do but stare ahead as the vines looped around his neck and head to form into a makeshift muzzle.

A tingling sensation brought Xavier's attention down to his own chest, his head able to move towards it as he saw the fur shift around and felt the sensation of touch on it. Just like what had happened when he tried to have the ghostly creature push into him the first time he saw the fur go from white to a light blue, and to his surprise he also saw the muscles of his chest thicken. He could feel his pectorals swell slightly as the invisible hands rubbed against them but before they had a chance to grow more the sensations ceased. The creature had pulled away but it wasn't because he was forced back like before, while there was some resistance the vines that had completely looped around Xavier's body were more than able to keep him there so the ghost could possess him.

As the bindings continued to keep Xavier completely immobile the kitsune began to have some second thoughts about putting himself into this situation, but as he felt the creature's presence behind him he knew it was too late for that. Suddenly there was a pressure against his upper back and Xavier let out a gasp of pleasure as the skin of his chest pushed out significantly, the bulge forming into the a face that looked like that of a humanoid shark as it stretched the increasingly blue fur underneath. His eyes widened in pure shock as he the head of the ghost had pushed his chest fur out so far that he could see the lips of the alien creature moving, something that would have probably terrified him if it wasn't for his previous experiences. Instead he found himself looking in awe as he felt the shark head shifted around inside of him and continued to cause his toes to curl in a bizarre sense of pleasure before it moved upwards as more of the ethereal body pressed up behind his own. He could feel something pushing up between the cheeks of his rear and Xavier found the alien to be clearly male, letting out a muffled moan as the ghostly cock quickly pushed up into his tailhole.

The body of the kitsune quivered within the restraints of the vines as a pair of hands joined the head that was still in his chest, pushing out his sides and stomach and making it look to Xavier like he was some sort of costume that someone was trying to get inside. The feeling of someone else inhabiting him like that was intense as more vines covered his body to keep him still while the possession continued. All he could feel was pleasure and he wondered whether that was from the body that Yavini had given him or something with the process that Nautlin was doing for him, but even in the areas where the creature hadn't pushed out was growing with muscle. The angular muzzle of the shark slid up into Xavier's head and as he began to feel a set of alien thoughts start to invade his own while the webbed hands of the incorporeal body had shifted to his arms and bulged out his biceps.

Xavier let out a muffled groan as the head pushed its way into his own, and as the ghostly muzzle pushed its way up he could feel his own start to transform. The vines that had kept him silent unfurled slightly as his vulpine maw began to grow thicker, feeling something grow against the back of his neck as he found himself unable to move his mouth and tongue. It felt like he had had eaten a scoop full of ice cream as the sclera of his eyes started to shift from white to blue. At the same time the metal lattice that the kitsune was bound too started to shake as Xavier's hips tried to thrust up into the air, not only from the pleasure that came from the ghost humping into him but also from the feeling of the cock of the creature sliding down from his stomach and into the shaft of the kitsune. Almost immediately his vine member thickened and turned a bright pink as the fur of his groin shifted in hue once more.

The vines continued to keep Xavier's body steady as his cock became rigid once more, losing the prehensile nature but gaining quite a bit of girth to it. By this point the fingers of the invisible creature slid down the furry forearms of the kitsune and towards his own digits, watching as webbing formed on it as they wiggled of their own accord. The kitsune continued to wiggle and squirm as his entire body thickened with a bit more muscle while he felt something press out from the metal behind him, a dorsal fin pushing out of his neck and back. His vulpine feet stretched out and turned to flippers and Xavier could feel his teeth sharpen in his maw, though he still couldn't move it since he no longer had control of his head anymore.

Even though Xavier was awash in the euphoria that came with their coupling he found his body relaxing, even his cock softening as he felt his physical form slump forward. With the tingling that suffused through his blue fur died down he could still sense the tip of his tail spreading into a fin while the vines began to glow around him. Once the transformed creature had finished the plants began to retract and slowly slithered off of the muscular form that was the hybrid of shark and kitsune. The one that set foot on the ground once more however was not the same person that was lifted off of it as a grin spread on the muzzle of the creature.

"It's been a while since I've been solid like this again," Nautlin said as Xavier felt his lips and tongue move, still able to see through his own eyes as he felt his body move towards the edge of the lake. When he saw himself he was surprised to find that he still had his vulpine ears but a very shark-like muzzle that continued to have a toothy smile as he turned to see his fin while rubbing on his furry face with his webbed fingers. "I see that the years have not diminished my swimmer's build, I was worried that being a spectral being would ruin my physique."

Certainly doesn't seem like it, Xavier thought to himself as he felt the spirit that possessed him flex his body. "I'm glad that you approve," Nautlin stated, causing the kitsune within to be surprised when he heard his own altered voice respond to him. "I can hear your thoughts and have gleaned a few surface memories Xavier, including knowing how you managed to get here in the first place. I guess I'm not surprised that Master Yavini was involved with your being here; he was the one that came to us in the first place to warn us of the solar storm that was coming and also gave us the means to protect ourselves."

So Yavini was involved in their transformation, Xavier mused as he felt himself start to walk around the pond once more. While it was bizarre not being in control of his own body the kitsune reminded himself that he had volunteered for this as the shark continued to explain what had happened that required them to be in that state. When their planet had been threatened with the solar storm the plant-loving people had actually managed to summon the nexus creature in order to help them, but rather than joining him in his realm as his minions they wished to stay with the gardens that they had cultivated. Thus an accord was stuck between them and Yavini created a special series of plants that carried their essence into their gardens, which the nexus creature was able to strengthen to resist the incoming solar flare, and was thus able to live on in that manner completely entwined and living with what they had created that was so important to them.

That was where Nautlin's problem came in; the sign that the solar flare was about to hit was that the skies would turn orange and the air would heat up, but in an effort to spread his own garden through the bottom of the pond where he lived he missed the initial warning signs while he was underwater. He had managed to get out and get the process started but before he could get the plants to reach maturity where he could join the others the solar flares hit and obliterated his physical form. He had managed to get completely within the plants to keep his essence safe, but without them reaching full maturity he hadn't been able to connect with the rest of the tribe… until Xavier came along and lent him a body to finish the job.

Xavier remained fascinated as everything was explained to him through his own voice as he continued to move back to the patch where he had first encountered the entity, though he was no longer the kitsune that had originally stood there. As they walked along the shore he continued to catch glimpse of himself and couldn't help but think that the hybrid he had become looked rather cute, especially as Nautlin seemed to notice his leering and flexed their combined muscles. But before he could think anything about it he found that the one possessing him had stopped in front of the patch of flowers and began to walk into the water itself.

"Well, it was really nice to meet you Xavier," Nautlin said as he waded their shared body until Xavier could feel the water lap up against his waist. "I'll see you on the other side."

Xavier wondered what the other creature meant by that, but before he could think about asking he felt something slither up around his legs that tickled against his finned feet before they coiled up his thick thighs and nestled themselves around his groin. Leave it to Yavini in order to make this the way that they fed their plants, Xavier thought to himself as he felt his muzzle smirk. There was nothing he could do as the vine slithered up and the hollow tip began to envelop the head of his cock. The smooth flesh practically suctioned around his stiff member as it slid down and the possessed kitsune could feel energy start to get pulled out from his body. It wasn't his own essence though and he could feel the other creature begin to drift down towards where the vine met his cock as the plants grew steadily around his form.

When the creature gasped from the sensitive flesh being stimulated there was a slight disembodied echo in their voice. Nautlin was using some of his energy in order to facilitate the transfer as the plants both on the shore and beneath the water started to glow. It was hard for Xavier to focus on anything though as more vines joined the one that had enveloped the throbbing organ all the way down to the root. A second one quickly began to push up between the thick, muscular globes of his butt and push inside and caused him to writhe in the water.

When Xavier groaned again he was surprised to find that it was his own voice that made the sound and as found he could open his own eyes and look down at himself once more. It was just in time to see the shark-like muzzle revert back to its vulpine state while the thickness of his shoulders and biceps began to deflate. He could also feel the webbing between his feet retract as he began to make little ripples in the pool from the vine milking him, while the one behind him pushed deeper inside. More essence was being siphoned from him and more than once Xavier could see a ghostly limb of the shark push away from his own body and looked almost opaque in the light. With the strength ebbing from his body the kitsune realized that it was the flowers themselves that were allowing Nautlin to manifest in this manner before several long pumps on his still huge member caused him to shudder in pure bliss.

As the last of Nautlin grew the flowers in the lakke and on the shore Xavier felt his orgasm quickly start to build. With more of his body under his own control it was getting harder to stay standing as he was penetrated further until the tip of it began to push against his own prostrate. That appeared to be the goal of this plant and finally it was too much for him and he flopped back into the water. As he floated there Xavier's eyes widened when he saw his still transformed cock within the confines of the tentacle and it seemed even bigger on his lithe body, though it was only for a few seconds until his back arched and he finally climaxed.

The pond and garden erupted into full bloom from the orgasm as Xavier added the kick of energy from his own nexus power that was still suffused with the last of Nautlin's essence that had been harbored inside of him. The kitsune panted heavily as his entire body once more belonged to him, feeling the water gently cascade against his skin as he looked around. He could see the other creatures of this garden forest more clearly now and especially the shark creature that began to swim around his new flowers. He could see Nautlin's form clearly now, and though he was still ghostly in appearance and gave him a smile before he swam forward until he went right through him.

"He seems to be quite grateful that you have helped him," Yavini said, Xavier quickly shifting his body around in the water to see the plant kitsune looking down at him from the shoreline. "I knew that you were the one for the job, and you have solved his plight quite gracefully."

“Glad you approve,” Xavier replied as he reached up and had the plant vine on the other kitsune’s body pulled him to the shore. “But if this was such a problem than why didn’t you help him? You were the one that got them to be like this in the first place, or couldn’t you just turn them all back to their real bodies?”

“My brothers and I aren’t gods,” Yavini replied with a bemused grin as he motioned for Xavier to follow him back through the woods. “Our power comes from those who desire things that happen to be in the sphere of influence that we operate under, and quite frankly to answer your most recent question the simple answer is that they’re happy the way they are now. Even if I could offer them their bodies I highly doubt that any of them would take such a deal, and with Nautlin’s problem solved I’m sure they’re going to all be perfectly content with where they are just as I’m hoping you will be with your new addition.”

Xavier tilted his head slightly in confusion before Yavini motioned with his head for the other kitsune to look behind him, and when he did he saw that he had grown yet another tail. This one had bright blue fur that was similar to the color change when Nautlin possessed him as it swished around in the air. Every so often the light seemed to catch it and it seemed to become ethereal in nature for a second before it reverted back to its normal form. Combined with the one he was born with and the extra one from his second task that made three, which Xavier knew would soon become more crowded as Yavini created a portal and ushered him to his next trial.

Chapter Four – Trial of Conquest

When Xavier reappeared once more he was surprised to find himself on a city street that was a stark contrast to the vibrant forests that he had been in. No one seemed to bat an eye at a three-tailed kitsune and when he looked down at himself and saw that he was also wearing clothes again. It was almost strange for him to be wearing such things as he made his way through the city in order to try and find who Yavini had slated for him to help this time. The problem was that there were so many people walking around that he didn't even know where to start. Was he supposed to find some random person off the street to help… no, that wasn't right, the last two he helped had very specific problems that were related to Yavini.

So something to do with plants then, Xavier thought to himself, but as the kitsune looked around he didn't see any plants either save for the weak trees that were spaced around the street. This definitely didn't look like a place that the nexus creature of plants would inhabit as he continued to walk. After about a block though he did see something that caught his eye; it was one of those hipster cafes that boasted about being organic and such, but what got the kitsune's attention was that they were also part of some sort of conservation network that had a large tree as its logo. It did seem that it would be in the vein of what Yavini would want and decided to head into the cafe and at least scope it out.

The second that Xavier walked inside he was immediately greeted with the smell of coffee. It was a rather small space that had a few tables inside of it and a small stage that took up a large corner of it, though no one was on it at the moment as he walked inside. There were only a few people that were eating and when he got to the counter there was initially no one there to greet him either. After a few seconds of waiting though a snow leopard appeared wearing a green apron with the logo of the café on it.

"Hey there man," the snow leopard said. "Name's Allen, what can I get for you today? We have a special on our tofu cheesecake."

"Oh, uh, no thanks Allen," Xavier replied. "I was actually intrigued by the sign out front that said you had a conversationalist group that you run out of this shop? I also wish to save the planet and bring a bit of green back to the city."

The snow leopard's face brightened considerably at this and the vapid demeanor that he wore vanished. "You really want to join our group?" Allen asked, Xavier nodding. "That's really cool of you man, normally I can't even get my vegan friends who come here to join in. Here, take a piece of cheesecake on the house and come with me to the back, that's where we meet up."

Xavier could sense that he was on the right track with this one and took the plate he was offered before following the feline towards the back door. As he smelled the dessert he was given the kitsune crinkled his nose and realized why it was on special as he tried not to gag. When they passed by a trash can he slid the contents into it and tried not to let the snow leopard see his suspiciously clean plate as they got to the door. He waited for a second as Allen unlocked the door and allowed the two of them to go into the back room of the café.

Most of it was filled with sacks of coffee beans and other ingredients along with a somewhat messy prep area that might be the explanation for the lack of customers outside. In one area of the room though there was a table that had a few posters with various earth-saving catchphrases on it as well as what appeared to be a number of plants growing in a small hydroponics shelf crammed into the corner. As the snow leopard launched into talking about how the cities were an unnatural blight on nature and that they needed to help nature reclaim it Xavier noticed that one of the plants was covered in a reflective glass case. When he walked over towards it though the snow leopard immediately went over and stopped him from touching.

"I would be careful with that one," Allen said as he put a hand on Xavier's shoulder. "That is a type of plant that we're breeding for a special purpose."

"What sort of purpose?" Xavier asked as he had a seat at the table.

"Like I said, we're going to help nature reclaim the city," Allen answered with an impish grin on his muzzle before he shook his head. "But it's not ready yet, and it's only as a last resort in case metahumanity can't change its ways. Now let me get you started with how the organization works and all the literature that we have printed out, as a warrior for the planet you're going to need to become very familiar with the cause in case anyone has questions."

Xavier could almost feel his eyes start to glaze over as the snow leopard began to show him pamphlet after pamphlet with everything from not eating meat to composting, the kitsune wondering in the back of his mind if these weren't causing more pollution than they were stopping. After about ten minutes though there was a shout from the front that prompted Allen to go and see what a customer wanted, the feline taking the rest of them and putting them in front of Xavier with the task to read them. When he left the kitsune glanced down at the literature he had been given before he slowly glanced back over at the plant that was covered up.

What if the one he was supposed to help wasn't the Allen or the ecowarriors, Xavier mused as he slowly stood up from the chair and walked over towards the hydroponics shelf. Yavini was the lord of plants, not creatures that were particularly fond of them, and strangely he could sense that he was on the right track with that line of thought. When he thought back to the snow leopard it was like he could see the desire of the feline wasn't to save the natural world, but to become a part of it. It was likely the entire reason in the first place that they created whatever was underneath the glass case that had piqued Xavier's curiosity in the first place.

After a quick look to the door to make sure the snow leopard wasn't coming back from what he was dealing with, which sounded like it was a customer that didn't like his coffee, Xavier slowly took the glass case and pulled it off of the shelf. What was underneath caused the vulpine to tilt his head in confusion; it didn't look like a plant at all, more like a bulb that was suspended in the water that hadn't even sprouted get. If this was what Allen was planning to take over the city he had a lot of work to go, Xavier thought to himself as he continued to look over the plant. The top of it was a bit open though and the fox wondered if it was about to germinate as he leaned his muzzle over it to try and peer inside of it.

Almost as soon as his nose was a few inches away from the bulb it released a puff of white mist right in his face. The surprise of the sudden action caused Xavier to inhale, and when he did his vision immediately began to blur and he started to feel like the room was spinning. The only thing he could hold onto was the hydroponics shelf and as he stared down at the bulb that had caused this condition he could feel his heart starting to pound and his breathing quicken. As the seconds ticked by his fixation on it only seemed to grow and as he slowly lowered his head back down towards the bulb an odd thought began to grow in his foggy brain…

…he needed to swallow that bulb.

Even though in the back of his mind he knew what was happening the thoughts never made it to his actual consciousness, and all he could do was watch as his own hand gravitated towards it without him telling it to do so. Within a matter of seconds he had plucked the blub from his holder and brought it to his muzzle, seeing something green poking out of the tip before it disappeared inside of his maw. The fulfillment of his sudden need caused a tremble of pleasure to go through his body as he quickly swallowed it, satisfying the urge that he had given. The second he felt it travel down his throat and enter into his stomach the dizziness and vertigo cleared as well, leaving him clearheaded enough to contemplate what he had just done.

It didn't take long before the three-tailed kitsune felt his stomach gurgle, pressing his hands against it as he began to feel something happening inside of him. While something like swallowing an alien plant bulb that he had been possessed to do should have made him nervous, deep down he knew that this was something that Yavini had probably already prepared his body for. Perhaps it was because he had been altered by the nexus creature that the bulb was able to do what it was fated to do, which to the vulpine felt like sprouting as he suddenly began to feel full. His stomach gurgled once more and as his hands pressed against his belly he saw the vines that were hidden in the thick fur of his forearms start to lengthen as though sensing the plant inside of him before he just took off his shirt.

At this point Xavier wasn't sure what to do as he stood there half-naked, though the bulb inside him seemed to know as his flat stomach began to swell with the plant matter inside of it. It was already much bigger than what he could normally contain and he wondered if it was because of his altered psychology or something the bulb was doing, either way he felt a spike of pleasure course through his body as the flesh around the growth began to push out. Snake-like bulges slithered out from it and went up his chest as well as down his hips, which only caused more arousal to suffuse through Xavier's system as the vines inside of him grew effortlessly underneath his skin. He could feel his limbs begin to tingle strongly and the tendrils that were already apart of his body began to lace together and stretch over his fingers, then continue to grow outwards as a moan escaped from his muzzle before he could clamp it shut.

Just as he could feel the vines start to grow up his back and through the muscles of his pectorals the door opened and the snow leopard walked through it once more. "Sorry that took so long, now as I was… saying…" Allen trailed off when he saw the shirtless vulpine standing there with vines sprouting from his arms and legs. "Oh gods Xavier, what have you done…"

“I didn’t mean too,” Xavier replied, though that was only partially the truth since he had been intending on releasing whatever was there anyway. “I can feel it growing inside of me really quick, you have a way to stop this though, right?”

Even though Xavier tried to sound like he was worried he could see that Allen was too freaked out by seeing vines start to spread over the concrete that had sprouted from the bulging feet of the kitsune as he put his hands on his head. “I… that isn’t even mine,” Allen said as he started to back away. “I’ll… I’ll call someone, the hospital, something-“

Both Allen and Xavier were taken by surprise as the lengthy vines that had grown from the fox’s arms suddenly darted out and wrapped around the feline’s body, coiling around him and pulling him forward. Even though Xavier was about to stop him from going outside anyway the plant that was spreading through his body had reacted to it faster than he could. The fox’s eyes widened when he realized he couldn’t control his outstretched arms anymore, just like when he had consumed the bulb in the first place, though this time he could sense the thought that caused it to happen. As Allen was brought in close Xavier could feel the vines pushing up through his throat and slithering into his skull, infesting his mind and driving him to its purpose as he leaned in and kissed the shocked snow leopard on the lips.

Allen tried to back away but the vines had already anchored themselves to his arms as Xavier continued to press their muzzles together, feeling an intense surge of need and arousal from doing so. This was what the plant wanted, the alien feelings mingling with his own as he took his tongue and pushed it past the lips of the feline. As he did he felt something bulge up into his throat and suddenly it wasn’t just his tongue inside, several vines spilled past his lips and joined his tongue in filling the muzzle of the other male. As their alien kiss continued Allen felt something drip down from between them, and though he had originally thought it was saliva he realized it was something thicker and stickier as he watched the shocked and confused look on the feline's face begin to relax.

With the snow leopard pacified and the infestation spreading towards him Xavier felt control of his body return to him again, though as he attempted to pull their muzzles apart he saw that both of them were stretched with a thick, wiggling band of vines that had already started to bulge out the throat of the feline. It did give the fox a chance to look down at himself and when he did he saw that his distended stomach had shrank back down, though at some point during his time dealing with Allen he had let his pants down. Vines were wiggling out of the underwear he wore and his own vine cock was already stretching it out as more of the bulb's tendrils snaked out into his tails and integrated with the ones of his legs and feet. He was also aware of the growing pressure of his mind to continue to spread as the vines on the concrete not only continued to grow but had also started to spread up the legs of the snow leopard.

But the point of the other creature wasn't to join him, Xavier thought as he began to feel tendrils push out of his nostrils that immediately went into the snow leopard's nostrils on his increasingly slack face. With the plant already growing inside the brain of the ecowarrior he could see the look change on Allen's face to pure euphoria. Part of the natural world, that was all he had wanted in the first place, and now he would serve it as a mindless drone to the plant that created it. Like a bee to a flower, Xavier thought, and soon his body would serve to spread the creature growing within it. But first it needed to get more incubators before it would make itself known, the alien creature controlling the fox and using the vines it had to render the snow leopard naked from the waist down.

Though Xavier found himself still able to think, a gift no doubt bestowed upon him by Yavini, the more the bulb guided his thoughts the more he got into it. His body was still transforming, mostly growing more vines that were starting to sprout from the body that hosted it as the vines and his own tongue retracted back into his maw. He had lost almost all control of his form, but unlike when he was possessed by Nautlin this plant had no intention of giving it back. As Xavier gripped onto the shoulders of the snow leopard he could feel his prehensile cock starting to push between the exposed cheeks of the other male, though what really caused a surge of pleasure to rush through him was the two vines that were pushing out of his nipples and wiggled in the air.

The vines that had grown up from his throat continued to grow out of Xavier's muzzle as his tongue transformed to join them, the kitsune unable to sense which was which as he noticed something wiggling against Allen's lips. The infestation had already taken hold of the other creature and soon he would be changing just like he was, but before that would happen the plant inside the host kitsune wanted to be sure their connection was secure. As tiny vines began to sprout from the ears of the snow leopard the vine cock slithered inside and joined with the others that were there, and as soon as it did Xavier suddenly felt a wealth of information enter into his own mind. The plant was able to access everything and anything from the new host and the kitsune himself could see that the earlier fear and shock had been replaced with the singular desire to spread and claim the city for the plant that was growing still inside of him.

With their neural link between the two parasitic plants established it dropped the snow leopard to his feet and commanded him to walk towards the door, tentacle cock still deeply embedded inside of his tailhole, and Xavier felt another wave of pleasure wash over him that radiated from the base of his groin. He looked down to see that a second vine cock had sprouted right next to the first one and as several others rubbed against it he found it was just as sensitive as the one that controlled Allen. By this point the table, the hydroponics bench, and most of the corner was being engulfed by the alien plant as he heard the snow leopard ask for several people that the kitsune host was able to identify as friends and fellow ecowarriors to come in. Almost immediately the plant pulled Allen back so that he wouldn't give himself away as they waited for the two to come in.

"Hey Allen, you cooking something back here?" the wolf that was the first to open the door commented as he came inside. "For once it actually smells really good."

"Yeah, my mouth is watering already," the horse behind him said as he came in as well, though he had to quickly stop when he nearly bumped into the wolf that had come to a dead stop just inside of the room. "Hey, what's the big idea?"

The wolf said nothing, mostly because Allen had already come around to his side from his hiding place behind the door and wrapped several vines around his body including his head. When the horse saw what was going on he tried to turn towards the door, only for the plants that had sprouted from the snow leopard's back to close it and start to grow over it to trap them inside. As the feline host looked at the one who had attempted to escape with eager eyes the equine gasped as he saw what looked like more plants growing out from his lips and curling around the muzzle that housed them. The equine ecowarrior continued to try and keep his distance from the infested snow leopard but as he kept his eyes on the feline he failed to see the tentacle cock of the kitsune in the corner until it had slithered into his waistband and pushed inside of him.

Inside of the kitsune host the plant reveled as two new creatures were delivered to it, the snow leopard taking the wolf and bringing him towards the mass of vines that contained the kitsune. More of the plant tentacles had emerged from the back, tail, and groin of the vine kitsune to the point where it was hard to see the vulpine within the plant that his body hosted. It didn't need to move much anyway though as it directed one of its vines to push into the equine's muzzle while the other one managed to snake its way into the tailhole of the shocked creature. At the same time the wolf had gotten his clothes ripped off, his own maleness erect and throbbing as the snow leopard that had gotten him naked began to push his own vine cock into the tailhole of the other male while one of Xavier's pushed into his muzzle.

Even though it was Allen that was inside the wolf's rear Xavier could feel the sensations as if they were his own, which combined with what he was getting from the one inside Allen himself as well as the vine that had started to spread open the horse was almost to the point of overload. That was probably the point of the plant, Xavier mused as he also began to feel the wolf and horse suck on the vines that were slithering into their maws, to keep their hosts stimulated and in the state of constant euphoria so that it could continue to spread. Part of him wondered what would happen to these creatures, but as the stomachs of the wolf and horse quickly began to distend and their cocks and tongues started to wiggle more than just by the throb of pleasure that coursed through them he found it harder and harder to concentrate…

As the four ecowarriors remained in the back the scene out front began to grow slightly more crowded from the other members of the conservation movement coming in. Since most people didn't come into the café after dinner they used the place as a meeting spot so they could plan where they would do their protests or any stunts for the weekend. As several members came in though they noticed that the snow leopard, as well as those that were usually hanging around, were nowhere to be found. With no customers currently in though they suspected that the three were just in the back and the large bull man went to tell them the rest of the group was there while the others waited.

"Do you think Allen would mind if I took one of his pastries?" a cheetah man said to the mare next to him as he stared down into the glass display case.

"I highly doubt he would even notice," the mare said in response. "I don't know how you can even eat those, even as the only vegan option in like two blocks you couldn't get me to try that after the last time I attempted to eat one of his brownies."

"Beggers can't be choosers," the cheetah replied with a smirk as he leaned over to fish out the pastry from the other side of the counter, only to stop and look down in confusion. "Hey, look at this."

The mare looked at the feline in question before leaning her head over as well to see that the floor was covered in what looked like thick plant vines that had started to grow up the counters and equipment. "Now that's odd…" she said as she turned her head to look at the others. "Hey, you guys got to see this, there's some sort of-"

"Weird plant growth?" the bear man near the stage interrupted, the mare nodding her head as she saw him standing next to an otter examining a busted air vent that had the same vines growing on it. "It's over here too, looks like those hanging vines on steroids. What do you think is going on back there?"

The mare shrugged her shoulders and watched the cheetah continue to pull himself further over the top of the counter in order to get at the pastries within until the door opened and the bull came out. With the angle they were at it was impossible to see what was going on in the back room as he came out and stood in front of her and the cheetah with a blank look on his face. "Hey, what's wrong?" the mare asked as the bull stood there silently. "What's going on back there?"

Just as she was about to ask again the mare heard a loud gurgle and looked down to see that the cheetah's maw was no longer filled with pastries, her eyes widening when she saw the bull was naked from the waist down and had his cock impaling the maw and throat of the outstretched male. As her eyes darted between the door and the bull she also saw that a thick, pulsating vine had stretched from it and was coiled up one of the legs of the muscular man before disappearing behind his back. Though she couldn't see it directly there was a counter mirror where she could see that the vine was slowly pushing in and out of his tailhole and that it was lodged deep inside. A sudden shout to her side caused the mare to turn her head and see that the otter had been pulled up against the vent by his tail and the bear was trying to pull him away.

When her mind finally unfroze from the sheer insanity of the situation she tried to run, only to find that the vines had spread from the counter to the floor and had rapidly curled up her legs. When she turned back to the bull she saw that his muzzle was stretched open by several vines that quickly darted forward and wrapped around her, the thickest one pushing into her maw while the others slithered into her nostrils and even her ears. As the plant infested the mare the bodies of both the cheetah and the bull began to quiver, not only from the pleasure being fed directly through the plant that corrupted them but from the plants that continued to sprout from their bodies. The shirt of both of them eventually ripped to expose the vines that grew from their chests and backs while the vine cock that pushed through the cheetah eventually wiggled out from between his butt cheeks as his tail grew and split into several more vines that latched around the mare whose eyes rolled back into her head like the others.

Inside of the back room Xavier hung there in his cocoon of plants as he felt more creatures being taken over as well as the café itself, the vine that was inside of the otter pushing all the way through and out of his mouth to infest the bear while the three at the counter continued to spread more vines through the café. They would all make for good hosts and as soon as they were ready would be unleashed upon the city to reclaim it, the ecowarriors fulfilling their true calling as the pants of the bear, mare, and cheetah all continued to bulge with new growth as the plants growing within them spread like wild fire. All that pleasure, not only from the hosts themselves but the parasitic plant as well, was fed back to the kitsune who wiggled in the vines that coiled completely around his form.

Then, just as he sensed the vines pushing their way into the neighboring buildings, the connection suddenly ceased and Xavier found his own eyes opening for the first time in a while. The vines that made up his own arms and legs quickly retracted back into his limbs and the others that grew from him slithered out of his body like snakes until he was no longer a part of the mass of vines that had held his body. As he slowly and carefully stepped his way out he looked around to see that none of the back room could be seen underneath the plants that had formed around every aspect of it, including the snow leopard and horse that remained completely still as the vines that emerged from their infested forms continued to grow and spread. It was definitely an odd sight, one that was growing more common by the second as he heard the sound of glass breaking and car tires screeching.

"Ah, mass conversion," the familiar voice of Yavini said as Xavier turned to see the nexus creature suddenly standing there next to him. "Don't get to do it very often, but sometimes the fate of a city is something that can be tweaked in your favor. In this case the idiot snow leopard over there that can't even make a cup of coffee was going to accidently release a biological agent that would have killed most of the city and the surrounding area, instead I was able to intervene and replace with something… a bit more fun."

"So instead of the entire city dying you turned it into a giant garden for a plant parasite?" Xavier asked.

"More or less," Yavini stated. "Nexus creatures only have the power to change those that are willing to be changed, which is why mass conversions such as this are rather rare and often draw the ire of the other brothers due to jealousy. It's also why I needed your help in kicking this off, something of this scale means I couldn't directly intervene, but a little replacement and a zealous kitsune attempting to earn a tail did the trick just fine."

Xavier was suddenly reminded of his tails and looked back to see that a fourth had indeed sprouted from his backside, though it looked more like a plant vine in a similar shape as the others as it wagged around in the air behind him. That made four tails, which meant if he really was going for all nine he only had five more to go before his journey was complete. It appeared that the nexus creature had more for him to do though and a portal was opened for him that they stepped inside so he could continue to gather.

Chapter Five – Trial of Internal Struggle

When Xavier emerged from the portal he was surprised to find that Yavini was still there with him and that the realm they had emerged into was slightly different than what they had been in previously. From just the feel of it something felt otherworldly about it, and as he looked up at the sky and saw a swirling of purple, blue, and red clouds he knew that something was definitely different about this stop. "I can see that you've already noticed that this isn't going to be your usual ordeals," Yavini said with a small grin on his muzzle. "While you've been out on our trials I've gotten word that one of my kin wishes to… share in the sponsorship of your journey, and I thought that since you have an affinity for his realm as well as my own we would at least hear him out."

A brother… that meant another nexus creature, one that was different from the lord of plants that he had been following this entire time. As the wind softly blew across the hill they were on while they walked up to the crest of it he wondered what Yavini meant by sharing. The plant fox had been entirely enigmatic since the two had met and though he had learned quite a bit already the fact that he was in the realm of another nexus creature entirely had thrown him for a loop. He could feel the four tails he had already earned shifting about behind him nervously as they got to the top of the hill.

Xavier's jaw dropped as he looked out over a sprawling manor that looked to be made of black latex stone, though that's not what his eyes were immediately drawn to. Creatures from all manner of mythology and fantasy were moving in and out of the manor while some lounged in the light that seemed to shine down from the clouds above. "These guys… they're…" Xavier said as his brain caught up with what he saw while looking at the glinting scales of the ones below. "They're all rubber…"

"Yes, this is my brother Renzyl's realm," Yavini explained as they started to head down towards the manor and the creatures that dwelled around it. "Just like my realm is foxes and plants, his is rubber and mythological creatures. I'm sure you can understand why we're here now."

Xavier found himself blushing slightly despite himself as he merely nodded in response. Though he greatly enjoyed the plant escapades he had been in so far he also had a fetish for rubber, something that both nexus creatures seemed to pick up on as he was led into the manor itself. While they walked he could see the minions of Renzyl give him a lustful look and could tell what they wanted, though a quick look from the plant fox himself made them quickly avert their gaze. It seemed that as long as he was in the presence of Yavini they weren't going to approach him, and as the kitsune looked some of them up and down he almost considered that a shame.

Eventually the two made their way through the manor and to the backyard where a large courtyard was constructed, complete with a marble dragon fountain in the middle of it. The entire scene looked idyllic in nature and with the all the muscular rubber guys around made it feel like he had walked into a dream. If it wasn't for meeting Yavini first he might have considered this to be a bizarre scene, but especially with his last trial it didn't faze him nearly as much after the initial shock. Eventually the two went into a small garden where Xavier saw a black rubber dragon and shiny silver raptor sitting at one of the tables, both with cups in their hands and two other chairs as though waiting for them to arrive. It was clear to Xavier which one was the lord of the realm as the kitsune and fox approached and got the attention of both.

"Ah, my dear Yavini," the rubber dragon said as he set the cup down. "How are things going in your realm?"

"Flourishing as always," Yavini was quick to reply as he looked around. "Seems your own little garden is coming along quite well, did you invite us to this spot just so I can see your progress?"

"Actually the reason is more for your little friend over here," the rubber dragon said as he turned his attention to Xavier. "But where are my manners; my name is Renzyl, sitting next to me is my second in command Chrono. Yavini tells me that your name is Xavier and that you're looking to become a full-fledged nine tailed kitsune."

"I suppose I am," Xavier said with a sheepish grin. "Wasn't what I thought I would be doing, but it's been working out so far."

"So I've been told," Renzyl replied as the smile on his face became slightly toothier. "Now the reason that I reached out to Yavini and had him bring you here is because while you do align more closely with his realm I sensed that you have a very strong affinity for what I have to offer, and so instead of you becoming a typical nexus beast we're looking to give you a slightly different path."

"Oh?" Xavier asked in curiosity. "What would I become?"

"A nexus hybrid," Yavini explained. "Several of our kin have started more collaborative efforts in order to see minions that can travel between realms, those who have exceptionally strong affinities for differing areas get the ability to be a part of both but not truly a minion of either. Much like the nexus beasts themselves you'd be operating outside of our realms and would share allegiance between myself and Renzyl."

"That… does sound really interesting," Xavier said as he looked up the shiny muscular forms of the two rubber males that sat opposite of them. "So… that means I would report to both of you or something?"

"You would be a shared agent between the two of us that we could both use as we please," Renzyl spoke up. "A slight priority would go to Yavini since you do align more with him, but you would help us more in projects that we plan together or utilize both of our spheres of influence. You would be surprised at how many people enjoy both rubber and plants and to be honest it's a decent mix."

“There would be additional responsibilities that come with being a nexus hybrid,” Yavini was quick to chime in. “Obviously keeping the trust of two realms will be more intensive than just one, but I’m sure you can imagine that the benefits would also multiply as well. This is your choice to make though, you can either choose to become a hybrid with Renzyl or you can continue on the path of being a regular plant kitsune with myself.”

As the three creatures stared as Xavier he suddenly found the weight of the decision he was about to make on his shoulders. From the sound of it he was being asked if he wished to indulge in his desire for rubber or if he wanted to remain solely the nexus beast of Yavini. As he glanced out of the side of his eye he could see that there were other rubber guys that seemed to enjoy gardening as well, but all of them were rubber and some sort of mythological creature which clearly made them Renzyl’s minions. He would be something different, something new, and as Xavier thought about it he found himself squirming slightly in his seat in anticipation.

“I mean, I’ve already come this far,” Xavier said as he gave them both a small nod of approval. “I’ll be this nexus hybrid of yours, a rubber plant kitsune sounds like a fun time.”

“Wonderful,” Renzyl said, turning to Chrono and giving him a nod that prompted the raptor to get up before he turned his head back to him. “Now as you were acclimated to Yavini I need to do the same to you, hence why we’re here, and since I don’t want to break your stride I’ve decided that you can help my minions out with one of their new projects while you’re here and get a new tail of yours.”

A new affinity and a new tail, Xavier thought to himself as Yavini and Renzyl got up and motioned for him to the same. They led him in the same direction that the raptor had gone off to and when they went through the wrought iron gate the kitsune found himself looking at a large greenhouse. The rubber dragon explained this was where the more temperamental experiments his gardeners worked on were housed and that what he was looking for would be on the other end of the building. Xavier nodded and tried to look inside only to find that there was a lot of plant matter that had grown up around it to make looking in almost impossible.

As Xavier turned to ask a question of the two nexus lords he suddenly found that he was alone, the kitsune sighing and scratching his head before he opened the door to go inside. Even though he was in the realm of one of the nexus creatures he had the feeling that he wouldn't get any help here, save for the direction that he had just been pointed too. When he walked through the threshold of the glass doorway he found that the greenhouse was much bigger than it looked on the outside, to the point where he had to crane his head in order to see some of the trees that grew up towards the ceiling. Fortunately the paths in the place were well-marked as he began to make his way towards the other end of the building.

It took nearly ten minutes for him to cross all the way and more than once he found himself jumping back slightly when one of the large mutant flowers or plants started to lean towards them. They were all shiny and synthetic in nature and would have looked fake it wasn't for the fact that they moved occasionally. Eventually he managed to make it to the other end and as he did he saw two green rubber lizardman that stood in front of a rather large plant with a bulb at the base of it. As soon as he got close enough the two immediately waved him over to stand next to them.

"Chrono told us you were coming," one of the lizardman said as he shook Xavier's hand, the kitsune noting the synthetic smooth texture of his palms before turning towards the plant in question. "We're really glad that someone was willing to help us out here, we're having a bit of a problem with our experiment and no one wants to volunteer."

"Volunteer?" Xavier repeated in question.

"Yes, this is our cross-breed of the hydrangea and anaconda flower," the lizardman stated as he gestured at the large base of the rubber plant. “At the moment we’re having trouble getting it to grow the way we wanted and so far the experiments have been less than fruitful, so to speak. We think that we managed to sort out all the kinks but we haven’t managed to get anyone to try it out yet.”

“I see…” Xavier replied as he continued to look the large stalk that emerged from the bulb up and down. If there was something additionally interesting about the plant he couldn’t see what it was so far, but he knew better after his last encounter to take anything for granted in these realms. “So what can I do to help?”

Xavier saw the faces of the two lizardmen light up as he offered to help them out and both gave him a big smile as they moved aside. “All you have to do is stand in front of it,” the one that had been talking to him said as he motioned to a patch of bare dirt right where the plant was. “Also don’t run or anything like that; we’re still working on its speed and other abilities so you could get away if you wanted, but that wouldn’t help us at all. Just relax and enjoy yourself.”

Though the kitsune knew that Yavini and Renzyl wouldn’t put him in any sort of harm’s way it didn’t make Xavier any less nervous as he took a step off of the path, something that the signs early on in the greenhouse specifically warned against, and began to make his way towards the plant. As he got closer he could see the end of the stalk was actually capped with buds like that on a flower, which started to shift when he got near. Once he had gotten to the spot that he was told to stand in he saw something push its way out of the end, Xavier gasping slightly when he saw it was the head of a rubber snake that had colorful petals that grew from its neck. As soon as he saw it start to lean down to him his first instinct was to step back but the kitsune made sure to steel his resolve as the large creature continued its approach.

Eventually the snake’s head was close enough to him that they were nearly eye to eye, and as Xavier wondered if this creature could actually talk he began to notice that the colors of the petals that framed the face of the rubber snake had started to shift around.

The pattern seemed to draw his gaze back in towards the eyes of the creature, and when he locked eyes with them he could see that the hues inside swirled around the serpentine pupils that stared back into his. When he realized this was some sort of hypnotic trap it was already too late; anytime he attempted to look away from the creature the petals brought his gaze right back to those eyes that continued to stare into him. Xavier began to feel his body become relaxed and his jaw grow slack as he leaned closer towards the large serpentine snout of the flower, his transfixed stare unable to look away as it became harder and harder for his thoughts to get past the swirling colors filling his mind.

Xavier wasn't sure how long he stood there practically drooling but eventually the hypnotic eyes of the snake-like creature disappeared, but the respite was short-lived as another series of flashing colors was shown to him. What the kitsune hadn't realized in his daze was that the snake had opened his maw and that the rubber of his insides had the same hypnotic patterns that drew him in, this time to the gullet of the creature. Without even realizing it he had started to move forward and put his head into the maw of the snake, too enticed by the colors to realize that he was essentially feeding himself to it. Eventually all he could see was the glowing hues that swirled around him as the mouth of the snake snapped shut and he found his feet lifted up into the air.

A vague, vulpine-shaped outline appeared in the stalk of the snake creature as the muscles contracted around Xavier, quickly pulling him down deeper while its tongue slithered around his furred form. The pleasure that came from the contact only served to deepen his trance as his hips disappeared into the snake and left only his limp legs and tails outside of its mouth. With most of his body inside though it didn't take much for it to swallow him down the rest of the way, especially with the powerful ripping movements that massaged his body and the slick insides that allowed him to slide down easily with the help of gravity. Soon the entirety of his form had been completely consumed and he was pulled down the stalk,

Xavier unaware of how much time had passed in his hypnotic enthrallment as he traveled down deeper and deeper…

After what seemed like ages his downward momentum was halted and Xavier found himself curling up slightly, like he was in some sort of pod or chamber as the glowing lights dimmed he found his mind begin to clear. With his enthrallment abating he realized that he was completely surrounded by rubber and though he was able to move it wasn't much more than the ability to adjust his position. As he felt his hands around for the opening he wondered if this was what those researchers were looking for, and if so what the exit strategy would be. He tired to find the stalk that he traveled down to get into it but there were no opening that he could find and as he pushed out more it felt like he was completely underneath the ground.

Eventually Xavier gave up in his attempt to actively escape and rested in the pod he had been captured in, idly wondering what the next step was. As he remained curled up the kitsune did find that it was an oddly meditative experience, reminding him of being in some sort of sensory deprivation tank as he continued to wiggle around. Perhaps this was the experience they were looking for, he thought to himself as he tried to remain calm, a means to completely pacify anyone that happened across their plant. With only the darkness surrounding him Xavier did find that he continued to see the colorful pattern in his vision, especially when he closed his eyes as he found himself relaxing even further.

As the kitsune started to drift off he suddenly felt the rubber contract around his body that caused him to snap back to attention. When he started to slide around inside the rubbery confines he realized that his body had changed and everything seemed… smoother, slicker against his skin. With his pod starting to shrink he only had a few moments to examine his own body and found that his fur had completely melted and was actually the same texture as the walls of the pod. Xavier remembered that Renzyl had mentioned he needed to become acclimated to being a nexus hybrid of plant and latex, which he now gathered was turning him into a rubber creature himself as he felt his body continued to get squeezed.

With his augmented physiology there was no need for him to breathe, but Xavier still gasped in shock as the rubber pressed over his face and was suctioned into his partially opened maw. At first he thought that it was a similar experience to a vac-rack or something of that nature, but as the chamber he was in continued to press in on him it felt like it was shifting and molding his body into something different, something new. It also had moved him out of the fetal position he was stuck in and straightened him out, pointing his head outwards as he began to feel his sides and chest stretch out in a very pleasurable sensation.

The combination of the hypnosis and the sensory deprivation had made it hard for Xavier to think of anything but the bliss that was being fed into him by the rubber, but as he continued to stretch upwards he found it harder to move his arms and legs. With his new synthetic skin he was able to at least rub his arms against his sides that they were pinned too and his legs against one another, but as his body continued to mutate it became harder and harder for them to even shift about. After a while he couldn't even feel his legs or his tails anymore and when he attempted to move them it was the rubber around his body that shifted about instead of his limbs. They had fused together, Xavier realized, and it wasn't long until his hands melded into his hips and the gap between his latex arms, sides, and the stalk itself was molded into one singular while he continued to shift upwards.

As Xavier began to feel himself push through the soil that he had been buried in the rubber of his face started to shift and warp, but what drew his attention even more was the changes happening to his groin. He let out a muffled groan as his cock had become fused to the same rubber the rest of his body as well as the pod itself, but as it did the sensation he normally got just from the sensitive flesh of his shaft seemed to spread out from that spot. The assimilation of his member had increased the sensitivity of the rest of his body to the point where the ground sliding against him was just like someone stroking him off as his vulpine muzzle continued to shift. The rubber that was suctioned up against his throat and mouth seemed to pull his face back until his muzzle was a rounded serpentine snout as he felt his tubular body wiggle back and forth in pleasure.

Finally the mutated pod broke through the ground and started to rise up in the air, but as Xavier's head continued to flatten and his ears melted into his skull the only difference that happened was the darkness had turned to a bright, green tinted light. As he recalled how the other plant looked he understood what had happened to him and slowly the outer covering peeled away as the last of his vulpine features disappeared. The second he was exposed to the air his forked tongue darted out past his lips as the rubber continued to sink down into his throat and into the rest of his augmented body. When the rubber creature tried to swallow it caused a shudder of pleasure and found that the material inside his throat had gained the same sensitivity of his cock just like his outer latex skin.

With the registration of that fact Xavier could see why the snake creature had been so interested in letting him wiggle and slide down inside of him, aside from creating another of his kind as he craned his flexible body and saw the stalk that contained the other hybrid flower behind him. "Mmmm, it appears that this one didn't flower either," a voice next to Xavier said, turning back to see the two lizardman researchers that had come up to examine him. "Everything else looks good though, it's just that one problem that we can't seem to replicate."

Didn't flower… as Xavier looked at his new body he found that his synthetic serpentine form that was outside the stalk didn't have any petals on it. That was the problem they were trying to have, the transformed kitsune thought to himself, they couldn't get the assimilated creature to germinate like their first creation. They were probably using other rubber minions to test, and as Xavier continued to see the tint of the swirling colors in his eyes he knew that he was no ordinary minion. If anyone was going to sprout it would be the one that called Yavini their master as the rubber plant snake concentrated and closed his eyes.

With the previous trials Xavier had learned what it felt like when the power of the nexus creature suffused through him, and while he might have been in Renzyl's realm he was still essentially a plant nexus beast. While the two beneath him continued to do soil measurements and rubber luminosity tests the rubber snake above them started to wiggle in the air as his body shifted once more. He let out a soft hiss of pleasure as he imagined a flower blooming with the same colors as the ones that were imprinted on his mind from his parent plant, and after a short while he could feel the rubber of his skin thicken before it separated into soft latex pedals. When he opened his eyes again they glowed with the same spiral pattern as the other plant and a grin crossed the new rubber snake flower's snout as he looked down at the two oblivious lizardmen beneath him.

Xavier waited patiently for the two researchers to be distracted and move in the proper position, and once their attention was both on his stalk he leaned back and lowered his head down to their eye level. It was clear from the shock on their faces that they hadn't expected to be face to face with his serpentine visage or the hypnotic coloration of his pedals, but even though they were aware of the peril of looking into his eyes the rubber plant creature smirked as he saw their gaze quickly zero in on him as their jaws went slack. "It appears that your experiment was a success after all," Xavier hissed as he waved his head back and forth slightly, watching them do the same as the vibrant petals continued to capture their stare. "Time for you two to enjoy the fruits of your labor."

With the two just as enthralled as he had been Xavier opened his maw and the two rubber lizardmen practically scrambled to get inside, the slightly bigger one going first with the other one right behind. The serpentine flower's lips began to stretch as he aided in the lizardman sliding down his throat, his tongue slithering around the midsection of the creature to pull him more in as he pushed down over him. As more of the reptilian creature disappeared inside Xavier couldn't help but wiggle and thrash about, eventually lifting the researcher off of his feet as the feel of rubber sliding against rubber made him almost orgasm right there. It was a surreal sensation that he couldn't quite describe, not only indulging in his new plant desires to create more seeds like what he had become but also from the sensitive flesh in his throat being stimulated by the lizard head wiggling around inside of it.

As more of the lizardman disappeared into the shiny tube of Xavier's body the former fox could tell that this one was very much enjoying it, especially when he got up to the creature's hips and felt something throbbing against his lower jaw. Though his intention was to take him one at a time he had an idea and looked over to the other enthralled creature that was still on the ground. He hadn't moved an inch and had also started to stroke himself while he watched his friend get swallowed up by their creation with a dopey grin on his face. Even with his mouth full the synthetic serpent flower lowered the still exposed legs of the other man down and put the hard cock of the creature right in front of the face of the other lizardman. To Xavier's pleasure the other rubber reptile quickly got the clue and took the thick shaft into his own muzzle, which only caused the one bulging out the flower stalk to wiggle harder.

Once the second creature had fully engulfed the member of the first completely in his maw Xavier slid his lips down further until the head of the lizardman was inside him as well. He could hear a muffled groan as the suction of his body kept the cock of the first lizardman inside of him and probably pushed it down even deeper as he was pulled up inside of the plant they had cultivated. For the serpentine flower not only was he getting pleasure from the ones that had started to slide down into his stalk but also seemed to absorb the lust from the two inside of him as the second one continued to fellate the first while they traveled deeper into his body. As Xavier tipped his head up and let gravity guide the humanoid bulges in his body travel down to be made into seed pods his body practically trembled from the sheer euphoria that he got from the act.

“Looks like someone is enjoying themselves,” Yavini’s voice said as Xavier turned his head to see him and Renzyl looking at him as they walked up the path. “And I don’t just mean the two that I can see having fun traveling down that stalk of yours. Seems like Renzyl’s researchers really do like to deep dive into their project.”

“They can be very dedicated to their work,” Renzyl replied with a chuckle as he put a hand against Xavier’s head and gave it a pat. “But we can’t have our new hybrid just lounge around here, so let’s get you back into a more proper form so you can continue your journey.”

Xavier nodded and began to feel the power of the nexus creature flow into him, and a few seconds later the secondary stalk that was his head and neck began to stretch out even further. He felt like he was being molded by invisible hands as he broke away from the plant that he had been connected to and felt his legs completely reform back into their original configuration before they even hit the ground. Being disconnected from the plant meant that the pleasure from the two was no longer being fed to him as his arms pushed out of his sides, but as his neck thinned and his head became vulpine in nature once more he could still sense them a bit as he turned back. By that point the two had disappeared under the ground and were being turned into two more pods that would eventually sprout up, but once Xavier had gotten his body back it appeared they were already moving on out of the greenhouse.

As the three walked Xavier looked down at his vulpine body and as he examined himself he was surprised at what he found. “Ah, you’re looking for the alterations that I might have made to your form,” Renzyl said, the fox nodding in response. “While it would have been just as easy to cover you in rubber and call it a day I decided to make your changes something a little more… subtle in nature.”

The fox saw the rubber dragon grin at him and then looked back down at himself to try and find what changed, but as he rubbed his fingers over his fur he realized that it felt… different in nature. As he walked out into the light of day though he immediately noticed an almost unnatural shine to the strands, a luster that he didn't have before. His body might still look like a furry fox, Xavier realized, but it appeared that he had been given the same synthetic treatment as most of the minions around here. As he turned around to look at himself though he did see one big difference to his body as his eyes widened at the new rubber tail that was actually a plant snake similar to his previous form.

"Don't worry, I'll teach you to disguise that aspect of yourself," Renzyl said as Yavini chuckled. "It won't take long, you do have a few more tails to gather up after all."

Chapter Six – Trial of Restoration

After spending some time in Renzyl's realm to get his tails to look uniform in nature the kitsune found himself leaving the rubber dragon and plant fox in order to continue on his journey for all nine tails. As a nexus hybrid Xavier found himself even more excited than before to see what would happen next; while he wouldn't tell Yavini the fact that rubber was involved as well as all the plant stuff had grown his interest even more to the point where he probably would have just accepted being the rubber dragon's minion. While he would have liked to remain in the realm longer he knew that he would have to go, just like he did when he first entered into the plant fox's domain. As he crossed through the portal to his next destination he could feel the five tails, which were now a uniform shiny green and vulpine in nature like the one that he had gotten from this realm, practically floating in the air as he did so.

When Xavier got to the other side he found himself in a place that looked like a village one would see in a fantasy movie, complete with straw roofs and dirt roads. When he looked down at himself his idea that he was in a more fantastical setting was confirmed when he saw that he was dressed looking like some sort of fictional warrior with leather armor and a few pouches that hung off his belt. Was this some sort of game world, the kitsune wondered, or were there actually dimensions that acted in this regard? Xavier mused that perhaps one was inspiration for the other as he began to walk into the village before he wondered who or what he was going to get involved with here in order to get his next tail.

It was clear that everything was very real as he felt the mud under his boots and several drops of rain that came from the clouds that gathered overhead. There were also a number of others both human and a few anthro that were around doing things like tending their gardens or just sitting about, some of them looking up and giving him a small nod as he passed by. It appeared to Xavier that someone in his attire was not out of place here either, though as he walked to the building he assumed was the inn the heavens opened and his thoughts immediately turned to avoiding being soaked. Though he failed in the latter regard the kitsune eventually got into the tavern and went inside, his clothes dripping wet as the water beaded off his synthetic fur.

The inn was just like Xavier had imagined when he first set foot in the world; a number of wooden tables and a crackling fireplace in one wall with a bar in the other. There were a few people within as well and as he passed by them he could hear general conversation happening that didn't seem to pertain to him at all. Some were talking about how the crops were doing and he wondered if perhaps that was supposed to be his queue, but if it was a simple farming task then why give him the strange warrior clothes? He remembered that sometimes in games there would be monsters that one would have to kill to save farmsteads… but that didn't seem like it fit the nexus creatures and he realized at that moment he didn't have a sword or any other weapon. It made Xavier feel slightly confused and decided to go over to the fireplace to try and dry himself off while he figured out a solution.

No sooner had Xavier gotten in front of the flames though than he saw someone approach him out of the corner of his vision. "Hail brave traveler," the man said, the kitsune looking the human up and down to see that he was in full plate armor and had a sword sheathed by his side. "If I'm not being too bold to ask, would you happen to be a wandering druid? We're about to partake of a quest up the mountains and could use the assistance of one that knows the ways of the natural world."

A druid… as Xavier looked down at himself again he realized that would make more sense than just some swordless warrior. Once again the offer made the kitsune think of game mechanics and guessed that this was where he needed to be and nodded his head. The human gave him a nod of approval and after introducing himself as Sir Willem brought him back over towards a table with several others around it. Aside from the warrior there was an elf that was dressed in robes that screamed mage and a large, brutish man that Xavier remembered in fantasy lore was called an orc. Once the warrior got the kitsune to the table he was introduced to the elf, whose name was Sparks, and the orc, who they called Bruiser, before having him sit down with them.

For a few hours the other three filled Xavier in on the fact they were going up to the caves and slay a dragon, and the entire time the kitsune wondered if Renzyl and Yavini were pulling his tails on this one. Casting magic and fighting dragons were the stuff of fantasy, though as the others turned their attentions towards a map that had been placed on the table he knew that dragons were in Renzyl's wheelhouse. As he thought about it though he had just turned into a giant rubber plant snake monster and could still hear the slight hiss of the rubber snake that was one of his disguised tails. Perhaps this was a way of teaching the hybrid that there were all manner of dimensions attached to their realms and that areas of high magic and fantasy were just like those of modern day cities.

Eventually the rest of the group wrapped up their plans and Sir Willem prompted them all to go up to their respective rooms to get a good night's sleep and that they would start at dawn. Reflexively Xavier spoke up and said he hadn't even gotten one himself yet and just as the warrior was about to say something the elf said that the kitsune could just bunk with him. The other two just looked at Xavier and since he wasn't even sure he had any money he accepted the offer and thanked the mage. After his sleeping arrangement had been settled the group parted ways with the elf leading the kitsune up to where he was going to stay for the night.

"You don't have a pack or anything?" Sparks asked as he took out the key and opened his room.

"I… travel light," Xavier replied as he looked around when he stepped inside with the mage. "So who gets to sleep-"

Xavier was suddenly surprised when the elf turned and pressed against him as soon as the door closed, his lips meeting the kitsune's muzzle. "I was hoping that we would meet someone like you," Sparks said once he had broken the embrace. "We're going to share this bed if you want to, and I won't say no to bit of magic practice either."

"I see," Xavier said, the kitsune using his nexus hybrid senses to realize that this elf really was quite adventurous as he stripped off his robe to reveal only a leather thong underneath. "You can count me in, though can I ask why you prefer, as you say, my kind?"

"Group met up with an evil druid a couple of months ago," Sparks said as he took his lean, toned body and laid back against the bed. "Naturally not the same situation as here but he entangled me in vines to keep me from casting magic. Still helped defeat him but for once I was glad for the robes so no one saw me fighting while completely stiff down there."

The kitsune couldn't help but smirk as he realized Sparks had hit the jackpot when it came to druids, but instead just gave him a nod and disrobed himself. Already the vulpine plant creature could feel the vines that were hidden inside of his arms start to extend outwards, this time not because he was transforming but to use them with someone else, and it was an opportunity that he wasn't going to waste. The elf let out a small moan of pleasure as the vines began to spread over him, coiling over the limbs of the other man and constricting gently around his skin while also coiling up his legs. When it got to his groin Xavier couldn't help but smile as he watched the rather impressive shaft of the elven male twitch and grow as tiny vine tendrils spread up it and began to stimulate the sensitive flesh.

Sparks muttered something about it being exactly as he imagined and Xavier shuddered in pleasure himself as his vines provided him with similar stimulation, but he quickly gathered this wasn't the trial. Indulging an elven mage in light bondage play was fun but it didn't seem to have the same impact as the other trials he had gone through and almost seemed too easy. Plus there was the fact that other than his vines being shiny as they looped around and pulled the elf's arms behind his back there was no indication of the other nexus creature's influence as well. The kitsune shrugged at this and decided that this would just be a bit of fun as he turned the elf onto his stomach and slid on top of him.

For the rest of the night Sparks became the plaything of the kitsune druid that Xavier had personified, pushing his cock in deep into the other male as he used one of his thicker vines to gag the elf. The other guy was practically putty in his paws and it wasn't long before those tight walls massaged the entire length of his maleness as he slowly thrusted in and out. With no external stimulation like being transformed into something or vines assimilating everything he decided to take it slow, his hands massaging the vine covered thighs and chest while his tendrils continued to stimulate the elf's throbbing cock. With his arms bound behind his back Xavier was able to move him around while keeping him fully impaled as he continued to slowly slide his entire length up to the hilt into Sparks.

After multiple orgasms the two eventually fell asleep against one another, waking up only when they heard the door bang and Sir Willem shouting for the two to get up and packed. Even soft Xavier was still inside the elf with their bodies bound together by vines and any fog of sleep was quickly dissipated when the other man wiggled out of his grasp after the plants loosened and his member was pulled out of him. "Well that was definitely a lot of fun," Sparks said as he tried to stretch, only for the vines to continue to hold him. "While this is definitely pleasing to wear I will need the use of my arms to help slay the dragon."

Xavier chuckled at that and was about to retract the vines completely when he got another idea that caused a grin to form on his muzzle. He did break the connection between his arms and allowed them free, but instead of pulling his vines back he instead shifted them around a bit and broke the connection between them and his arms. The elf looked down at himself in shock as the vines formed into a harness and cuffs with smaller tendrils that curled around between them. He looked like a dryad, Xavier mused as the bulk of the smaller plants formed something similar to a jockstrap that caused the mage to quiver as it contained his erection.

"Not sure if this is a gift or a curse," Sparks said with a chuckle as he cupped his groin, feeling it twitch underneath the vines that occasionally shifted to arouse him. "I'm certainly glad for wearing a robe, perhaps that will be all I wear. Will make it easier for tomorrow I'm sure when we celebrate our victory."

Sparks gave Xavier a kiss on the muzzle and went to get on his robe, and as the kitsune got dressed as well he wondered if he would even be around tomorrow. Most of the time his sojourn on the various planes of existence were short-lived, perhaps as he gets more tails the trials become more complex in nature he mused. The last one did involve him getting essentially eaten by a giant plant snake, a lot of trust on his part, so perhaps this one would have another virtuous aspect attached to it. It was a lot of speculation on his part but for the moment he seemed to be exactly where he needed to be as he got dressed.

Once he and Sparks were ready to go they joined up with the rest of the group that had gathered downstairs; after breakfast they left the tavern and started to make their way up the mountains. It had stopped raining but everything was still quite wet and caused the group to stumble more than once as they made their way up towards the cave that Sir Willem implored was the lair of the beast. Despite the trials of having to climb up a muddy hill though there wasn't much in the way of monsters or creatures that needed to be killed, something that Xavier was grateful for. More than once however he was asked to use his divine magic in order to tell them where to go, and though the kitsune faltered at first he realized he could use the power Yavini gave him to sense things through the plants and directed them to the largest void in the trees that they hiked through that probably indicated a dragon's lair.

After a few hours Xavier was relieved to find that he was correct in his assumptions as they happened upon a rather large cave, Sir Willem cautioning them all before he drew his blade and moved forward with the rest of the group. As they moved into the darkness of the cave the kitsune wondered if he was actually going to have to kill a dragon, or this was going to be part of the trail that he was going to have to undertake. He didn't seem to have any actual powers other than what Yavini and Renzyl have granted him and he still wasn't sure what else the latter had given him other than rubberized fur and augmented physiology, so he wouldn't be good in a fight against some feral beast. If it was a creature that could be talked to however perhaps he could use some of his gifts in order to make it so they all got together?

When they got to the very depths of the cave however Xavier and the rest of the group saw there was not going to be a fight at all as the light of the lit torch their warrior held fell upon the bones of a dragon. "Hey Willem, how old was this information you got again?" Bruiser asked with a slight chuckle as he patted the stunned man on the shoulder. "It seems we're a few years late to the party, someone has already done the slaying for us."

Xavier couldn't help but laugh at that as the group began to spread out and look for treasure that might have remained after the passing of the dragon they were supposed to have taken out themselves. The large cave broke off into several smaller tunnels and the kitsune watched the others fan out in order to try and find some means to make the journey worth it before he went to the skeleton itself. It certainly was quite the beast, he mused as he looked at the large teeth of the skull that were almost as big as his arm, and imagined it would have given this group a very large fight. He carefully crawled over one of the large forearm bones and looked inside the ribcage of the creature and was surprised to find that there was a large puddle of liquid was inside…

…a shiny black puddle.

Was this perhaps the essence of the dragon, Xavier wondered as he moved over towards the puddle and examined it more closely. It was something that any cautious explorer would probably avoid, or take a sample of and leave it be, but as he was not an ordinary adventurer. As he hovered a hand over the pool it seemed to stretch up to meet him, and though he easily kept his fingers away from it he found that the dragon was in fact within the puddle he was on the edge of. He could sense that the dragon wasn't just some beast at all but a part of the natural world; when he had been killed it through everything out of balance which caused the plant life to wither and die in the area, and with the dragons in other areas being driven out as well there was no one to be the stewards of the world around them.

Dragons were basically druids, Xavier mused as he looked up to make that no one else was there. Not only did this connect with plants but he was guessing that the liquid wouldn't lose its rubbery nature as he stood up and quickly took off his clothes. Fortunately the others had gone off in search of what fortune remained of the dragon's hoard and no one could witness his naked body stepping into the puddle of liquid. The substance was fairly warm and even before he could get to the middle of it the goo started to travel up his body as Xavier felt the essence of the dragon thank him for what he was about to do.

As Xavier watched the thick black goo travel up his ankles it reminded him a bit of his trial with Nautlin, but as it flowed up his calves he knew this would be slightly different as he felt his feet begin to warp. Not only did they start to swell with new growth but he could feel the actual appendages start to become… softer, like they were being turned into the same goo that had already gotten up to his knees while his calves bloated out with new muscle. It appeared to the kitsune that his transformation was not just going to be to a different species this time as the rubbery substance flowed through his already synthetic fur, especially as he saw the still unassimilated parts of his legs swelling before the goo even touched it as tentacles pushed up within his skin while converting everything underneath.

Xavier began to wonder he was going to start melting into the puddle itself; but it appeared the goo he was becoming would be firm enough to keep him upright as his feet finished morphing into something far more draconic in nature. He gave a little bounce on the newly formed appendages and despite their gelatinous nature he could still stand on him, though his knees quivered slightly as the goo reached his groin and began to push into his tailhole. The kitsune quickly clapped his hands over his mouth to keep from making a noise as the tentacle slithered up inside of him, causing his already covered member to grow erect while joining with the goo that already had cascaded up into his stomach. He could see his body rippling from the changes as everything from the waist down looked like he was covered in thick tar that continued to creep upwards on him.

It was clear this dragon was no stranger to pleasure as it decided to thank him by stimulating his prostate while the goo around his erect shaft thickened. Xavier had to hold onto one of the nearby dragon bone ribs in order to keep himself steady as it felt like a maw was sucking him off while his stomach molded into washboard abs and his pectorals inflated. As the pleasure continued to suffuse through his system he looked back to see his tails had also morphed into more draconic appendages, but he still had five of them as a pair of gooey wings began to spread out from his back. As the thick substance reached his mouth the transforming kitsune couldn't help but let out a moan that turned to a gurgle as the goo that transformed his insides pushed out his mouth, nostrils, and ears to meet with the liquid rubber assimilating his outside body. As his head was completely enveloped Xavier could feel a pair of horns grow out from behind his ears and watched his vulpine muzzle stretch and warp, which didn't stop the smile from forming on it as he realized he still had a connection to his plants…

Meanwhile in another tunnel Bruiser and Sparks had found that the ones that they had gone down separately joined together and continued to explore for loot while talking. "Can you believe it?" Bruiser scoffed. "Got my armor muddied for an already dead dragon and an empty cave."

“I feel bad for our new druid companion,” Sparks replied. “Dragged him up here and he led us to this place, how are we going to give him a cut if we don’t get one ourselves?”

“Maybe you can treat him to another night in your room,” Bruiser said with a coy grin on his green lips, which caused the elf to blush and turn away. “Thought I was the only one that got to split the cost of a room with you.”

Sparks said nothing in return, only motioned for the orc to continue forward as he leaned up against the wall. Partially it was from embarrassment that came with his fellow adventurer and lover knowing that he had slept with the kitsune, but the main cause was that one of the vines that cradled his firm butt cheeks had started to slide up inside of him. Had the druid decided that since there was no threat they could have some fun, he wondered as the vines around his growing cock began to move once more. Part of him wanted to find the other man and tell him this wasn’t the place, but he wasn’t even sure he could move as the vine began to slip inside of him and stretch him open.

Had the elf taken off his robe he would have seen the green vines start to darken, particularly the ones around the makeshift plant jock he wore that turned to a deep black. He tried to take a step forward to keep up appearances with Bruiser but the tentacle was growing thicker and pushing in deeper, sliding further inside than anything else as he let out a soft gasp. It also felt like his cock was growing bigger and stretching out the mesh of plants that contained it, and when he reached down to grab it his eyes widened at the size. He had always been big for an elf, which was why the orc ahead of him fancied him in the first place, but from the feel he had grown at least a few more inches and the sensation was enough to take off his robe to examine himself.

Bruiser had continued down a few more feet before he realized that the elf was no longer with him and when he turned back he was surprised to find that Sparks had taken off his robe and stood there almost naked, with one notable exception. “Oh wow, the druid really did a number on you," the orc laugh as came back while watching the black plants at his groin stretch out with something huge behind it. "You going to be his little bitch now where he can play with you however he wants?"

"It's not funny Bruiser," Sparks shot back, though it was punctuated with a moan as his cock finally seemed to push out of the bulge that contained it that caused both men to look in awe. "Look at me, I'm huge! What magic is this?"

"Something I can get behind," Bruiser said as he stepped forward and leaned in front of the throbbing cock, watching the shiny black member continue to alter and warp as it grew a tapered tip and ridges along the length. "That druid might have the right idea, and since you can't seem to help yourself with this new cock of yours…"

The orc trailed off and though the elf wanted to say that it was because of the growing tentacle that was stretching his backside impossibly while ramming his prostrate all he could do was moan as the other man took it into his mouth. Though it was large and completely erect it still had a softness to it that allowed the orc to slide it inside somewhat easily, shifting it between his tusks as Sparks grabbed his head from the sudden pleasurable sensation. Had either been looking they would have seen the elf's stomach begin to stretch from the tentacle thrusting inside of it, which the elf thought was a particularly thick vine but was actually his new rubber tail spreading him open. As the mage's transformation was hastened by the blowjob being given to his rubber goo cock his feet scratched into the stone from the talons growing out of it, Sparks pressing his hands against the skin of his belly as it began to turn black while growing more distended with each thrust.

Finally Sparks let out a loud yell of pure pleasure as his gooey body could no longer contain his tail and it pushed out of him completely as the cock inside the orc surged with new growth and stretched down into his throat. Before Bruiser could react from his neck bulging out and feeling claws suddenly touching his scalp the tail of the mutating elf pushed against his head and began to coat the outside of his face with the gooey tip. While the body of the mage was swelling with muscle from the changes happening inside it the orc's head was morphing from the outside first, the combined rubbery ooze being fed to him pushing out his face into a draconic muzzle as a pair of horns grew from his skull that Sparks immediately latched onto.

Even though he still had some semblance of control of his body Sparks was too enraptured in his lust to care, and he could feel the tendrils of the dragon that had been slain here starting to root in his mind while he thrusted his growing hips into the maw of the shiny dragon-headed orc beneath him. While the creature that had made this place its home until it died wasn't going to take them over, the kitsune behind the strings making sure of it, they would be the new guardians of the natural world. Xavier couldn't help but smile as he could feel the face of the elf begin to stretch out as though an unseen hand had started to pull on his jaws while his nose melted into his face to become a pair of draconic nostrils. It helped for the two having sex before to speed the process up and it wouldn't be long before there were two more rubber goo dragons that made this cave their home.

That just left Sir Willem. As the original gooey dragon brought his mind back from the transformation of the elf and orc Xavier saw the human had just come out of the cave that he had been exploring and stood there with his sword drawn while looking at him furiously. "I should have known!" the human said as he got into a fighting stance. "A druid comes in our time of need, were you in league with this dragon or was this just an opportunity?"

Xavier just shrugged his muscular shoulders in response, imagining that seeing a thickly muscled anthro dragon in shiny black rubber goo was probably a shock to him in the first place. "I guess you could call it opportunity," Xavier replied. "A chance to restore order to the natural world after someone like you came in and killed this creature."

"I see…" the human said with a sneer as he brought up his shield. "Well I'm not sure how to kill you, but we're certainly going to try."

"I think you'll find that there is no we anymore," Xavier said as he licked his rubbery lips. "You'll find very soon that your friends were more than willing to choose this life for themselves as well, and I think they'll have no trouble convincing you of the same."

There was a momentary look of confusion on the warrior's face before he was suddenly attacked from behind, his sword and shield dropping to the ground as a huge rubber goo dragon came up behind him and locked his arms. As Sir Willem shouted and cursed to be dropped instantly a second smaller creature came up to his front, this one with a very intricate harness system over his whole body that caused Xavier to smile. The one known as Sparks before his transformation leaned forward and pushed his rubbery tongue into the mouth of the human as the rest of the vines on his body unfurled and began to push their way into the warrior's armor.

"Not bad for your first excursion into the realm of the hybrid," Yavini said as Xavier turned his head away from the human whose armor was being flooded with transformative goo to the plant fox that suddenly appeared beside him. "Whether they continue to spread and create a whole new race of druid-like rubber dragon creatures or just remain here content in the cave of their predecessor is up to them, for you though we need to move you on to your next task now that you've gotten what you came for."

Xavier looked behind him as his body suddenly warped back to normal, seeing a black rubber tail that was in the shape of a dragon. Much like the others he could give it any form he want and made it vulpine before nodding to Yavini. The two glanced once more at the three adventurers, a goo dragon with thicker rubber plates like armor being spit-roasted by the other two while still wrapped up in the latex vines of the former elf thrusting into his maw, before the nexus creature opened a portal and led them through. Just as they disappeared Xavier wondered that if this was how he got his sixth tail then what the last three trials were possibly going to be…

Chapter Seven – Trial of Emptiness

Xavier stretched his body as he found himself in an entirely new place, still remembering his gooey form and shivering in delight from it. While being the black ooze dragon and taking over the other three to become ones as well was fun he knew there was more that he could do with such a power. He had gotten used to Yavini and the transforming of others through plants and with the rubbery creature he had just become in his last trial he was excited to continue to combine with Renzyl's ability as well. As he took note of his surroundings he found himself at some sort of campground and saw that like the last place there were humans and anthros alike, though this one clearly had a more modern day setting as he looked at the RVs and campers that were scattered about.

A prime spot for plants, Xavier thought to himself as he began to walk about, but he wasn't sure exactly what he was going to find for the rubber aspect. When he got to the middle of the campground he saw that there was a lake as well as some woods that were nearby, it reminded him of the moonbloom flowers and the florescent plants as well from his previous trials. Perhaps this was going to be another werewolf that he needed to help, the kitsune thought as a smile appeared on his muzzle as he remembered how he got his second tail. It didn't take long as he reminisced before he found two humans that sat at the pier, and since they were the only ones that were out and about and not sitting around a campfire Xavier decided to investigate.

As he approached the two he could see that one was in distress and the other was practically in tears, which caused Xavier to pause when he assessed the scene. Was it possible that he had made a mistake in who he was supposed to approach? He felt like that wasn't the case but he still felt himself hesitate before approaching the two and instead tried to listen in on what they were saying instead. It was hard with the wind rustling the leaves and the background noise of people laughing and talking but eventually he got close enough to hear what had caused the problem in the first place.

Even though he could only catch the occasional word from the one that was freaking out he could hear that the reason they had come down to the dock and on the camping trip in general was to try and get the first man to overcome his fear of water. An interesting problem, Xavier mused as he pretended to look at the rules that were posted on swimming in the lake, and one he wasn't sure how to rectify. How would he be able to use plants or rubber, or plants and rubber, to get someone to no longer fear doing something like splashing around in a lake? It wasn't something he was going to solve on the outskirts of the problem and the kitsune decided to try and insert himself into the situation instead to see if he could get a better handle on things.

"Excuse me," Xavier said as he approached the two, watching the one that was having the panic attack try to quickly compose himself in the presence of another. "I was just passing by and saw that you were in a bit of distress. I don't mean to stick my muzzle where it doesn't belong but I just wanted to see if everything was alright?"

Though Xavier could sense a bit of apprehension of a stranger coming into their business he could see that the one trying to give the comfort was at least grateful for the distraction. "It's nothing serious," the taller man said. "We have a pool party that we were both invited to but Kyle here had a bit of a bad experience with the water and can't even get close to it without breaking down. I thought that maybe coming out here and trying that thing where you expose them to their fear might help, but it's been two days and so far we haven't even gotten him to get onto the beach yet much less the water."

"Dude!" the other man said as he put his hands to his head. "Why would you tell him all that?"

"It's alright," Xavier quickly said to diffuse the situation. "I don't know you two or anything so it's not like I'll spread the word, and maybe I'll have a way to help you in order to alleviate your fears. Just give me a few hours and we'll come back at sunset to try it, alright?"

As the two men discussed the offer Xavier took a second to look them over and try to assess how to help. They were both younger, probably either at the tail end of or fresh out of college, and from what he sensed of their desires they were definitely down with being with each other in a carnal way if they hadn't been already. The one problem was that there was nothing he could sense that would involve plants or rubber that he could latch any of his powers onto in order to make this work. The other man, whom Xavier eventually gleaned was named Francis, loved the water and Kyle really did have an intense want to overcome this fear of his to join him at the pool party.

Pool party… a bolt of inspiration came to the kitsune at that moment and he had to hide the smile that formed on his muzzle as a plan started to form on what he would do to the two. It would involve a little work on his part and some scavenging. but fortunately he had given himself a few hours to do it as the two humans agreed to meet him back at the pier at sunset. Once they had broken off Xavier immediately started to forage for supplies, eventually finding what he needed near a couple of RV's that were parked near the lake itself. He felt a bit bad for what he had to do to their rubber items, but as he got what he needed he found that being a nexus hybrid of Renzyl meant that he could infuse the material with his power and warp it to suit his needs, a skill that the kitsune knew was going to definitely come in handy in a few hours…

Eventually the sun set and the two humans once more found themselves on the dock, looking around for the one that told them to meet here. "Are you really sure about this?" Kyle asked as he looked over the water nervously. "What if he's some sort of criminal?"

“Do you really think that this guy told us to come back here in a few hours so he could mug us?” Francis replied while he gave his friend a dour look. “Even at night this place is completely lit up including the pier, so unless he drags us out into the middle of the lake to murder us I think we’ll be fine. Plus there’s just something about him that seems trustworthy, like we can depend on him in order to solve this problem.”

“I certainly hope so,” Xavier said as he stepped onto the dock suddenly, causing the two to jump at the sudden appearance of the kitsune who gave them a small smile. “Sorry if I startled you but I just finished up something that I think would help. But first to make sure that I’m on the right track I would like to try something first.”

The two men looked at one another and when they turned back Xavier took the glass of water he had been holding behind his back and splashed it in Kyle’s face. Francis looked in surprise as Kyle sputtered and wiped the liquid off of his face as it dripped down his shirt and soon his pants. “What was that for?” Kyle practically shouted before the other two told him to quiet down.

“Wanted to make sure that it wasn’t just a fear of water itself you had,” Xavier replied with a shrug. “I suspect that you actually have a fear of drowning given your friend saying that you had a traumatic experience, which is a perfectly reasonable phobia, so my solution is to make it so you feel impossible to drown.”

Xavier could feel his tails practically twitching in anticipation as he held out the item that he had spent the entirety of his time alone creating, the two looking at the air nozzle that was held out to Kyle. “Is that… for me to breathe through?” Kyle asked as the eyes of the two continued to stare at it as though waiting for it to do something. “I don’t get it.”

“We’re going to put this on you and get you to think like a pool toy,” Xavier revealed. “If you believe that then you will go on the water and any worries about drowning will vanish. What do you think?”

The grin on the kitsune began to fade as he saw the apprehension in both guys, but especially Kyle as he shook his head. Their connection to rubber or anything like that wasn't strong enough to get over the barriers that kept him from getting into the idea, Xavier realized as they began to say that it was a little weird and they probably weren't interested. Though their willingness was high their inhibitions kept them from embracing the concept that was being floated to them, and as the kitsune wondered how to get around that he heard a hissing sound come from behind him. As he looked back he saw that the tail of his which he had gotten from the snake plant had gone back to its original form and as it raised up over his shoulder he suddenly saw the eyes of the two humans were drawn to it.

Xavier looked back at the two and as he waved that particular tail back and forth he saw them move with it, which prompted him to smirk as he saw their postures begin to relax. "I think that it's just a matter of perspective," Xavier said as he kept the snake head close to his own so the two also focused somewhat on him. "You two seem like you're willing to try new things, and you want to get over your fear of water, right?"

Both Kyle and Francis nodded with a slight prompt from the snake head and Xavier could practically see those roadblocks that prevented the two from having an open mind melt away before him. "So in order to do that Kyle needs to think that he's a pool toy to give him the confidence to float on that water," Xavier reinforced as he held out the nozzle. "All you have to do is take this nozzle and get into the mentality, your head filling with air to allow you float all those negative thoughts away."

"Yeah…" Kyle said as Xavier took the hypnotic tail and disguised it once more, which caused both to snap out of their impromptu trance while he looked down at it. "Just feel lighter… I think it's working already. Where do I put this?"

“Well, one thing is for sure,” Xavier replied as he went over and tugged on their shirts, taking advantage of their suggestable state to push things further. “Pool toys typically don’t have clothing.”

Once more the two looked unsure as they looked around but Xavier once more whipped up the snake tail to get their attention. “Perhaps the pier is not the best place for a couple of pool toys to hang around,” Xavier said as he watched their features go slack immediately while he looked around the lake until he found a small beach set into the woods. “You two follow me, I think I know a place where we can both get comfortable.”

As Xavier put the tail away again he saw the two nod enthusiastically and follow him along the shore to the partially hidden cove. One thing the kitsune didn’t want to do was oversaturate them to the point that they were completely enthralled, though as he glanced back at them the excited nature of the two and the fact they had to turn and adjust themselves more than once meant that they were very much into the concept. It was always surprising to see what gets dug up after removing the surface layer that prevents them from enjoying themselves, Xavier thought to himself as they got to the cove. The kitsune hoped that one of the desires was about to be unearthed as they stopped in the small lake cove and he once more told them to disrobe.

This time the humans did what they were told and in less than a minute both stood there on the beach completely naked. While he only had one nozzle Xavier figured it would be fine for the friend to participate as he told Kyle to pick a spot and put the object against it. The kitsune had an idea of where he might put it and as expected it went straight to his belly button, pushing it into the crevice where the rubber fused with the skin unnoticed. Since both humans were still in a light trance from his snake tail Xavier once more began to tell Kyle that he was a pool toy and that his mind and body were becoming lighter, thoughts drifting away as he saw the skin around the nozzle began to turn a shiny green.

"I can really feel it," Kyle said as Xavier began to guide him to the water. "I'm really a pool toy."

"Yes you are," Xavier confirmed as he led him down to the water. "When you step into the water you'll feel it press up against the rubber of your body, but while you'll continue to feel the sand and stone as you walk in you know that at any time you can just lie on your back and drift off. Go ahead, take a step in."

Kyle nodded and as soon as his human foot was immersed into the water the flesh turned to rubber and became semi-translucent in nature. The transforming human made it a few steps in before he stopped and lifted his foot in the air, wiggling the webbed feet that they had become as he reached down and squeezed it. "It's real," Kyle affirmed as he squeezed his foot and saw the air inflate the calve that had also turned hollow and rubber with a fin decoration coming out of it. "I'm... a pool toy... a sea serpent pool toy."

Xavier was impressed as Kyle took control of his own transformation, opting for something aquatic in nature as he stepped forward more into the water until he was up to his waist before backing up to see the changes himself. The first thing the kitsune noticed was that Kyle's maleness had grown in length and become more like a tentacle, wiggling around despite just being an air-filled rubber tube essentially. The big change however was the tail; Kyle had backed up before it finished forming and the other two could watch as it grew out from the rubber of his rubberized backside, a spine running down it that started to grow up the still human flesh and assimilate it while a pair of hard rubber handles formed near the base. While any other human would have freaked out but for the corrupted human it was something he always had, and though Francis looked dumbfounded in shock for a second the reality warping mental changes also caught up with him and he splashed in to hug his friend.

"I knew you could get your true form back," Francis said as he squeezed the half-pooltoy half-human creature, watching his legs swell from the pressure as he looked down at the throbbing rubber cock pressed against his stomach. "I'm jealous that you get to float around all day like that and I have to stay like this. Don't suppose you mind me getting a ride on you?"

Xavier could already tell that the lusts that come with such a transformation were clearly getting to both of them and the kitsune decided to step in once more. "Well you know that a pool toy can turn another into a pool toy as well," Xavier said as he planted the seed into their hypnotically influenced brains. "But that's going to require Kyle getting a ride from Francis instead of the other way around."

"Oh… I see…" Francis said as he turned back to Kyle, whose chest and stomach had become the sculpted body of an athlete after being coated in the smooth green rubber. "Kyle, you think you could… do that for me?"

"Of course I can," Kyle replied with a grin, which began to grow longer as a muzzle started to push out from his lips while shiny green splotches appeared where his nose started to melt into his face and his ears stretched out into fins. "I'd do anything for you, and you got me here in the first place. The least I can do is return the favor, and if that means spreading you open than that's just an added benefit."

Definitely had done this before with each other, Xavier thought to himself as he watched Francis turn himself around and let the sea serpent pool toy get behind him. By the time the tapered tip of Kyle's cock pushed in between the cheeks of the other male there wasn't a trace of his human flesh left, and from the look of it his fear of drowning had been completely erased as well. It didn't hurt that he no longer needed to breathe as well as floated naturally while the pool toy shifted himself so he could use his newfound flexibility to suck the cock of the one he was about to change. Blue rubber began to quickly spread over the thighs of the other man as Xavier could see the cock of the human inside the serpentine snout stretching and transforming already as it shifted down into the throat sleeve of the synthetic creature.

As Xavier congratulated himself for another job well done he was about to step out of the water before he heard the voice of Francis call out to him. "Hey, you're not going to duck out on us, are you?" Francis said as he waved an arm towards the kitsune, which had turned the same shiny dark blue as his thighs as the skin started to stretch out from the lengthening limb to form into a pool toy handle. "You were the one that helped show us the light, the least we could do is let you get a taste of the pool toy life."

The sea serpent pool toy pulled off of his partner and looked at him, and as Xavier heard the squeaks of their rubbery bodies as one humped into the other the kitsune noted that neither Yavini nor Renzyl were there to take him out of the situation like they usually did. After a few seconds of mental deliberation he decided to enjoy the fruits of his labor and sloshed back over towards the two, only to be immediately embraced by the wing arms of the second pool toy that had been created at that lake. They weren't going to simply let him float on them, Xavier gathered as he watched the human's face push out into a more draconic snout while a pair of horns inflated from his head. Despite the two being nothing but air and rubber they were surprisingly agile and soon he found himself in between the two with their unnaturally smooth, air-filled forms pressed against his synthetic fur.

First Xavier and Kyle's muzzles met in a kiss and it wasn't long until Francis joined in, and as the kitsune found his mouth filled with two squishy rubber tongues he found himself accidently pressing in too hard to Francis and his muzzle completely pushed inside of it. The scene caused the two to chuckle but the new pool toys were not just satisfied with making out as the two sets of arms groped and squeezed against his body to heighten his pleasure while they pushed their erect members against his body. After they splashed around with a bit of foreplay Xavier found himself on all fours with the water level right at his sides as the green sea serpent pool toy went in front of him while the blue sea wyvern floated around behind him. The two were more than eager to have the kitsune join him and it showed from the thick member that pressed up against the side of his muzzle while he felt another one slide against his thighs.

It was probably one the first times that he got this involved after he had helped out those in his trial, Xavier mused to himself as he opened his maw and licked his tongue around the shaft of the man in front of him. Whether this was some sort of reward or his benefactors were running late he didn't care as Kyle suddenly shifted forward and pressed the tip against his lips while the wings of the wyvern pooltoy pressed against his hips and sides. What caught the kitsune's attention the most however was that his tongue began to feel unnaturally smooth and as he continued to stick it out to lick around the shaft of the sea serpent he saw that it turned a dark green rubber and looked like the appendage that was starting to push into his changing maw. The transformation was already starting and as Kyle began to push in more insistently Xavier began to literally feel light-headed while his skull was transformed to rubber and air just like the two that he was between.

It didn't take long for Francis to follow suit as the wyvern pool toy pushed up underneath Xavier's tailhole and started to push past the rubber ring of muscle and into his body. As both cocks slid into him at the same time the changing kitsune couldn't help but be impressed at how firm they were; even though there was some transference of air as he clamped down on both sets inside of him there was only a bit of squeeze to it while the rest continued to fill him out. As he felt his tailhole start to get stuffed he could feel his cheeks begin to transform and allow the sea wyvern to penetrate further into the one beneath him. Xavier could feel his own maleness start to grow as well and it wasn't long before it lengthened to the point that it started to press into the water, though it was pushed back up to the surface as it became the cock of a pool toy just like the others.

Xavier let out a muffled grunt as the sea serpent slid into his throat, stretching out his neck before it pressed against something that slightly surprised both of them. The bright green cock could still be seen in the increasingly translucent rubber of the kitsune's throat as the sea serpent still managed to hilt himself inside. As his vision became tinted with dark green and he could feel the rubber cascading down his shoulders as well as up his waist he realized that like the others he had to keep the air in somehow and that both his throat and tailhole would be sealed at the end of the passage in order to keep the integrity of his body. Soon enough the sea wyvern also bottomed out inside the kitsune pool toy that was being created as Xavier looked at the reflection in the water to see the bright blue shaft inside his dark green body, as well as a pair of handles that morphed out of the rubber skin.

Soon Xavier felt his arms and legs give out from under him and realized he could float there effortlessly as the rubber fur of his body melted together while most of his insides had already been converted to air. The sound of soft squeaks filled the atmosphere as the kitsune could feel the rush of pleasure not only coming from the two cocks sliding against his synthetic insides but also just from his own body bobbing up and down in the water of the lake. Even with his vision mostly taken up by the bright green abs of the sea serpent he could still see himself with the last of his old body disappearing into the dark green patterned rubber of his new pool toy form. Even his tails joined in as they became inflated as well, falling around the sea wyvern as Kyle grabbed onto the handles that formed onto Xavier's shoulders and thrusted it hard enough to partially push in the vulpine muzzle.

One thing that Xavier realized he still had though was his vines, though they were hollow rubber tentacles at this point, and smirked around the mouthful of serpent cock as he grabbed onto the handles of the sea serpent's thighs. Kyle had been so enthralled with watching his new inflatable body thrusting forward into the floating toy in front of him that he didn't even notice the tentacles until they started to push into his tailhole to cause the same pleasure that he was giving the kitsune. Both his and the sea wyvern's eyes widened, though they didn't have eyelids since they were pool toys, as Xavier did the same with his feet tentacles to the rear end of the other man behind him as well. Soon the only thing that could be heard was the splashing of water and the sound of latex rubbing against latex as the kitsune pooltoy took advantage of their physiology to stretch them open with several tentacles while a few more drifted up and played with their maws.

Eventually all three had their share of orgasms that caused the two that were still standing on the shoreline to fall backwards, pulling out of the vulpine as they began to float on the water of the lake themselves. With the intense sensations from being spit-roasted and the climax that came from it subsiding the kitsune pool toy had a chance to look at himself for the first time while the other two continued to drift about around him. Even though he felt solid and could sink himself down into the water he also found floating to be effortless as he tugged on one of his handles and felt a measure of pleasure come from it. He used his own vines to coil around and squeeze his biceps and chuckled slightly when he saw his hands grow bigger, though he wasn't able to depress the rubber more than a few inches before the resistance was like that of a regular body. As his focus went down to his cock that was now exposed in the night air he gave it a few strokes and found the rubbery appendage just as sensitive as before.

Though he was tempted to go another round with himself Xavier heard splashing about that caused him to look up in question. The two had managed to drift out further into the lake had used their wings and webbed hands to try and get the other wet as they laughed in jubliation. It was clear that the phobia of drowning in Kyle had been cured but as he watched them move further and further away from the shore he wondered if perhaps this wasn't the proper solution after all. Though he had already dealt with people turning into werewolves and vines that took hosts to spread through a city these were just two guys that were now pool toys in a world filled with normal people.

"I wouldn't worry too much about that part," the voice of Renzyl said suddenly, which caused Xavier to flop over in surprise and flip over to where he was face down in the water until the rubber dragon used a handle on his shoulder to hoist him to his feet.

"Didn't mean to startle you, but as for your concern that this world won't accept them I can assure you that they will either find the means to change back to their old forms or, more commonly, reality will be rewritten in their favor to make it so that they were always pool toys."

Xavier thought back to the conversation that the two former humans had at the start of their transformation and through his tail's hypnosis convinced them that they were pool toys in the first place as he looked at the two still splashing around. "I can't imagine that you could hypnotize the entire population," Xavier stated, which caused Renzyl to laugh and shake his head. "Then it's hard to believe that the world will just warp around them to cater to the needs of two guys that wanted to have fun at a pool party. Yavini told me that your kind aren't gods."

"That we aren't, as much as some of my brethren like to think otherwise," Renzyl responded with a smirk on his muzzle. "But what we do is cater to the desires of those in the world, and we often find that the universe will correct the rules of the realm rather than try to change back those that have gotten what they truly wanted. Maybe someone out there wishes to see it happen, or that the nexus hates a paradox, but either way they won't be the first to find themselves suddenly in the world of synthetic creatures and its highly doubtful they'll be the last... or I may just snatch them up and bring them to my realm as minions."

Renzyl motioned for the kitsune to follow him back towards the shore and as Xavier did he found that his new attributes were already starting to revert back to normal. The dark green rubber practically melted off of his body as fur reappeared and he started to feel heavier after the antics of his pool toy form. By the time the two stepped back onto the shore the kitsune was back to his original state, save for a new air-filled rubber tail that was the last remnant of his pool toy self, as a portal opened in front of him. He realized as he stepped through that he only had two tails left and could only wonder what the next challenge was going to be…

Chapter Eight – Trial of Companionship

As Xavier found himself in yet another new world the seven-tailed kitsune found himself immediately taking stock of the situation as he looked around. This time he found himself on some sort of farming community as he saw several buildings surrounded by various crops. The area was rife with potential as he felt his plant fox powers tingling from everything that was around him. At first he thought it might just be one farmstead that was in the area but as he walked down the street further he could see that it was actually a small village.

It made him wonder if he was transported to another area in the past or a fantasy realm until he saw a human man drive a car down the dirt road he was walking on. Definitely more modern era, Xavier thought to himself as he continued to walk down into what could best be described as the center of this small farming town. Just like the last few times he saw human and anthro alike, and though he got a few looks it appeared that his multiple tails weren't unheard of either. It made him wonder if the nexus that Renzyl talked about made it so that he could come into places like this and not have to worry about hiding his identity as he looked to who or what he could possibly help for his trial.

Since it was around the same time of night as when he had left the campground there weren't a lot of people around and it made Xavier wonder about the next clue. With a lot of farms around he assumed that it would have something more to do with plants than rubber, especially since his last one dealt with exclusively the latter with the pool toy transformation, but that might not necessarily be the case. His first few trials were all about Yavini and perhaps Renzyl was making up for lost time, which continued to tick away as the people that were out became less and less before finally he found himself the only one left that walked around. Without a watch or any sense of time the kitsune had to guess that it was getting to the wee hours of the night and not only was there nothing pointing him in the direction of his trial but he started to feel like he was sticking out as a stranger in this community while he wandered the streets.

Just as Xavier began to think about trying to find a hotel or something for the night the starry sky suddenly lit up with a flash which blinded him for a few seconds. At first he thought a bomb had gone off but as he looked up in the air he saw something that was on fire streak down towards one of the fields that bordered this small town. The kitsune followed the trail all the way down before it landed with a fireball that lit up the night once more as the ground trembled under his feet from the impact. Several car alarms could be heard going off and as Xavier glanced at the houses on the street he could see that the noise and vibrations had caused a number of people to awaken.

As people began to go out of their houses Xavier suddenly felt compelled to run to the site of the crash, especially as he had been the only one that saw where it landed and though he could see smoke rising up from the impact site he also began to feel droplets of rain against his head. He hadn't realized how cloudy the sky was even with the meteor streaking through the air and as he got to the corn field it landed in he suddenly found himself being soaked to the bone by the rain. The thought that this was too much of a coincidence that he would be the only one to see it weighed on him as he found himself surrounded by the tall stalks. After a few minutes he had to stop as he could no longer see the smoke of the site as the rain grew heavier, but just as he began to feel lost he suddenly felt a ping with his plant senses of something that was far different than the crops that surrounded him.

Eventually Xavier had to stop once more, but this time it wasn't because of the corn but the lack of it as he suddenly found himself at the lip of a crater in the field. Surprisingly despite the size of the fireball that landed the hole was relatively small, maybe a few feet down and twice that in diameter, and instead of a large rock there was an alien flower that grew up in the middle of a puddle of glowing green goo. The strange substance looked thick and viscous and with the two combined together Xavier knew exactly who he was about to help as he made his way down towards it.

"Never thought I would actually be helping in an alien invasion," Xavier said with a chuckle as he took off his clothes, knowing they would likely not be needed anyway. Even before he got close to the edge of the pool he could see the alien flower's petals spread and it move towards him. "Seems friendly enough, though that bulb did too and it's probably spread those vines through most of that last city by now."

Xavier wondered if this town was about to fall under a similar fate or if whatever alien consciousness he was about to interact with had other ideas, but he wouldn't know until he actually made contact with them. As soon as he stepped into the thick goo he could feel it completely coat his foot, though when he pulled it out instead of being a radioactive green it was a sleek, shiny black instead. Definitely has rubber involved, Xavier thought to himself as he watched the flower continue to move towards him. At first he thought it was about to clamp around his face but instead it went lower, the pistil in the front of the plant sliding over the tip and shaft of his cock before the petals latched around his groin while a wave of pleasure cascaded over his body.

Already he could feel the suction sensation on his shaft causing it to grow bigger as rubber seeped out of the flower around his groin and began to drip down his legs while he was being sucked off. Xavier could feel his legs buckle slightly as the pleasure from the flower intensified, and as the kitsune tilted his head back to let out a moan it turned into a gasp as something got pushed in between the cheeks of his rear. As he turned around it was just in time to see another rubbery flower that had risen up from the goo and began to push inside of him. The kitsune practically grabbed his stomach as he felt the tentacle-like appendage slither into him and whether or not the alien had a means to make it pleasurable Xavier was glad for his augmented physiology as something large and spherical inside the vine of the flower that was latched around his backside suddenly stretched him wide open.

The sudden rush of intense pleasure caused Xavier to finally fall backwards, splashing into the thick goo as the object that was now sliding through his synthetic inner walls traveled to his stomach. When he raised his arms up again he saw that his dark green synthetic fur had been completely replaced with solid black rubber, and though his vines were blocked inside of it he began to feel tendrils spreading from the alien plant. Even though he was being turned to rubber the alien creature was seeding him like a plant, a fact that become all the more obvious as the one that had started to piston in and out of his tailhole had finally deposited the object inside of him to push out the rubber flesh just above the base of his cock. When he was able to stop thrusting his hips upwards from the stimulation that was being given to him by the one sucking on his growing cock he could inspect the lump that had formed in his abs, an alien seed that would soon be joined by others as a second object being pushed up his taihole by the vine inside him caused Xavier to hump upwards once more.

Soon only Xavier's head remained above the glowing green goo, but as the two flowers humped into him with one bulging out his stomach he knew that it wouldn't be long before he was completely taken over. He could already feel the alien creature inside of his head, whispering to him and altering his thought patterns to corrupt him into its way of thinking. Anyone else probably would have tried desperately to fight this creature to the bitter end, but the kitsune knew that they were probably on the same page when it came to what they wanted. Nevertheless Xavier didn't just roll over and give up control, but eventually the pleasure became so much that he could feel himself losing his mental footing… though that didn't matter much anyway as the glowing substance began to leak out of his nose and ears while also drooling out of his muzzle before he slowly sank completely down beneath the surface of the alien goo…

For a few minutes the only sign of activity down in the crater was the occasional disturbance of a vine pushing upwards as Xavier was completely inundated with the alien species. The second his head had slipped under the rubber it had pushed inside his skull and taken him over, reminding him of the bulb that sprouted the vines but in reverse. He had kept his psyche completely intact though as the plants of that scenario just wanted his body to continue to spread, this alien was far more intelligent and methodical as the kitsune felt his thoughts and instincts being remolded into what was needed. This was no mere alien plant, this was an invasive species as the arm of the kitsune briefly broke the surface of the goo only for it to slowly sink back down as tiny vines spread through the thick black rubber.

After an hour the goo and the plant contained within it suddenly started to break down. A thin layer of water had built up from the rain that was coming down on top of it before the service tension of the liquid alien rubber broke and seemed to soak into the soil. Everything quickly drained away leaving only two things in that crater; the dead remains of the alien plant and the rubber kitsune that laid in the in mud. As he laid there his rubber cock, which had grown to nearly a foot in diameter, twitched between his synthetic legs as the creature slowly regained consciousness. Multiple orgasms and the will of the alien leeching into the mind of the kitsune had eroded away Xavier's psyche and when the eyes opened to reveal glowing green orbs it was a different creature who looked through them as he slowly got to his feet and silently walked out of the crater, alien plants sprouting where the green goo that leaked out of it touched the soil...

The next morning the farmstead whose cornfield got hit all came out to see the sun shining with only the wet grass an indicator that it had rained the previous night. With the storm coming in so soon after everyone heard such a loud boom they all suspected that it had just been a bolt of lightning that hit someone's field, and since there was nothing to indicate to the contrary that anyone could see it meant the da would go on as normal for those who left their various houses to tend the massive acreage that belongs to the various families that live in the farmstead. For two friends, a minotaur named Ollie and a snow leopard named Archer, that meant that they had to go out into the fields and do a check to make sure that the rains hadn't started to drown any viable crops. Though both were considered the young'uns of the group they were both in their mid-twenties and had been friends their entire lives as they slogged through the wet dirt.

"I think they just do this to us on purpose," Archer said as Ollie stopped to wipe his brow and take a drink from the canteen that he usually hung from his horns. "All this time we spend out here when we've already made sure that there is adequate drainage. I think that they just don't know what to do with us."

"I can think of worse ways to spend the day," Ollie replied as he flexed his beefy arm before extending the canteen out to the snow leopard. "You'd think with all the hauling and walking you do it'd put a little more meat on your bones."

"Not all of us can come from prime bull stock like you," Archer said with a chuckle after he took a drink from the canteen while he looked out, though he stopped when he seemed to notice something in the distance. "Hey, what is that…"

It took a second for Ollie to see what his friend had seen and the two got up from their resting place to check out what the snow leopard had found. When the two got up to it they both stopped short of the plant that was growing out from the ground between the stalks of corn as they both tilted their head in confusion. "Is it… some kind of weed?" Ollie said as he leaned down and poked the stalk of the strange flower. "It's got an, ah, interesting look to it."

"It looks like a penis flower," Archer replied, which caused the minotaur to snort as he backed away from the phallic plant while the snow leopard to chuckle. "What, I'm not going to spend all day out here beating around the bush, and that's what it looks like. Hey, I'll give you ten dollars to suck it."

"Oh shut up Archer," Ollie replied. "That thing could be poisonous for all we know."

"Maybe to your reputation," Archer said with a grin before it turned into a frown as the bull stamped his foot to the ground. "Don't be a chicken, I promise I won't take any pictures or anything. Plus it wouldn't be the first time I saw a dick in your mouth."

Ollie felt himself grow flushed with embarrassment as his friend mentioned their flings out in the middle of the field, something they had stopped when they almost got caught by a passing trailer. It had been a few months and though the minotaur didn't say anything about it, even though he was extremely pent-up. "Hey, I seem to remember that you're the accomplished cock-sucker around here," Ollie shot back. "You suck it first, and then I will."

"That's a deal," Archer replied quickly as he knelt down in front of the phallic flower. "I expect you to hold up your end of the bargain by the way." The minotaur couldn't help but snicker as he watched the snow leopard take the fleshy stalk and put it in his mouth, looking straight up at Ollie as he gave it a lick. Though it was supposed to be a joke the bull man couldn't help but shift his overalls as he felt them tighten slightly in the front from the feline fellating the plant in front of him.

Just as Ollie was about to grab his phone to take a picture though he heard something that caused him to pause. It was just along the other side of a small hill that crested near them, which was one of the reasons they were there in the first place, and with his tall stature he didn't have to go far to look over it. What he saw when he took a few steps and glanced over it caused him to gasp and back up, nearly knocking into the snow leopard who had started to bob his head up and down on the plant while making lewd noises. Though Ollie couldn't be sure he thought he saw some sort of fox in a latex gimp suit thrusting a huge rubber cock into Bertrand, one of the neighboring farmers, who not only had his pants down but some sort of flower pressed against his groin. At first he thought that his own horniness was making him see things but when he heard a low moan from the other side of the hill it seemed to confirm what he had seen.

Ollie whispered to Archer for him to get up and that they needed to leave, but as he heard another muffled grunt from where he stood he saw that Archer had completely impaled his muzzle on the flower until it was practically pushing out his throat. As the minotaur reached down and told him in a slightly louder voice to stop playing around he saw the feline's face suddenly widen and as Ollie pulled him back Archer sputtered and coughed. "I think that thing just jizzed inside of me," Archer said as he spat out a translucent green slime. "That was gross."

Before Ollie could say anything they heard a louder moan from the hill next to them and as they looked up they saw the glowing green eyes and black rubber heads of two creatures staring down at them. The minotaur shouted for them to run and the two quickly made their way through the stalks of corn in order to try and lose the two that were likely pursuing them. Fortunately they knew the fields like the back of their hands but as they passed by the markers that told them where they were in relation to the rest of the farmstead Ollie wondered where that second creature had come from. His anxiety increased as he thought back to the two and saw one fox while the other was a rubber ram that looked somewhat like Bertrand…

After a few minutes Archer and Ollie slowed down as they got closer to the edge of the cornfield, wading slowly through the crops to see if they had been followed. It appeared they had lost those strange creatures in the field but as they approached a small clearing in the corn where their water tap was they heard something that caused them to duck down. At first they thought it was the two that were following him but as they looked closer they saw that it was one of the other farmhands, a muscular horse man who had stripped down naked and appeared to have one of those phallic plants spreading open his tailhole while another one was latched against his cock. He was muttering to himself how good it felt while tweaking his nipples and as he pulled up his hips they could see something round inside the stalk that traveled up into him.

What really caught Ollie's attention though was the shiny black substance that seemed to already have coated his lower body. At first it looked like the veins of his legs were popping out from underneath the rubber but as the horse grabbed the flower with one hand and stroked it against his throbbing tool, which was massive from the look of it when he accidentally pulled it off a bit, they could see that whatever was inside him wiggled like snakes. Eventually the horse seemed to cum and as his back arched in the air glowing green goo leaked from both his tailhole and where the plant was on his cock, which caused more strange plant vines to sprout up that wrapped around his hooves and slithered into the rubber of his body that caused it to swell with even more muscle. The two were rendered speechless as more of the glowing goo dripped out of the stallion's mouth and where it made contact with his body the alien black rubber spread over his head while his eyes began to glow green.

Just like what happened with Bertrand, Ollie thought to himself as he pushed Archer to stop staring at the transforming creature and continue to move. Eventually they got out onto the lawn of the farmstead but as they looked out to the street they saw that whatever was happening hadn't just kept itself to the corn field. Several large rubber creatures had vines that sprouted from their synthetic bodies wrapped around others, keeping them in place as they either had their own cocks inside of them or allowed more of the phallic plants that seemed to be sprouting up from the ground to penetrate their orifices. It wasn't just the farmhands either, as Ollie and Archer snuck around towards the minotaur's home they saw a muscular rubber wolf gimp with his feet dug into the garden while vines slithered out to the ground… except as the bull watched the lupine creature stroke his cock he knew that it used to be a wolfess that lived in that house who owned the nearby bakery.

As more of the alien rubber creatures seemed to appear out of nowhere Ollie and Archer realized they were trapped; the main road was crawling with the monsters and the crop line wasn't safe either with all the farmhands being converted. As Ollie looked around he saw one of his neighbors, a tiger dairy farmer named Michell, was waving over to him from his storm cellar. The minotaur got the snow leopard's distracted attention and pointed to the tiger, then the two of them snuck over as best they could while crossing over exposed lawns. Fortunately it appeared that the creatures were more concerned with their lusts than being on the lookout as they got to the doors and quickly went down into the cellar as Michell closed them once they were inside.

Both Ollie and Archer panted heavily as Michell deadbolted the door before going down the stairs to them. "Anyone know what the hell is going on?" the tiger asked as he looked at the two. "Was just about to go into my barn to milk the cows for the day when I saw two guys in what looked like rubber suits just going to town on one another! Didn't seem to notice me and I ran back to the house, which is good because I saw one of them pounce on Davis and by the time I got in through my door some weird plants and that rubber was spreading all over his body."

"You know as much as we do," Ollie replied with a shrug. "We were out in the fields and came across Bertrand and some fox gimp that we never saw before, next thing we know we have two rubber guys coming after us. Do you think you could call this in?"

"Cell tower is dead," Michell replied as he showed his cell phone with the words no service on it. "Let's just stay put for a second and think this thing out."

Ollie nodded and as he looked around the cellar for anything he could use to help he glanced over at Archer, who had taken a seat on some crates while holding his stomach with his arm. "You alright?" Ollie asked as he walked over. "You don't look so hot."

"Just not used to running for my life in the sun," Archer replied with a smirk before giving the minotaur a dismissive wave. "I'll be fine once I catch my breath and get rid of this stitch in my side, hopefully we can get out of here before those things get us."

Though the minotaur nodded he gave his friend a look before going back to his search, though as soon as he turned his back the snow leopard took his other hand and adjusted the front of his pants while he sat up. Ollie found the storm cellar not to be very big but it was packed to the brim with shelves full of old stuff that the tiger might have used at one time or another. There didn't appear to be anything of use though and after he went around each section once he headed back to the main area to see what Mitchell and Archer were doing. As he got to the last set of shelves he could see the tiger working on something on the nearby workbench and Ollie couldn't help but notice that the feline had removed his shirt to expose his very well-muscled body.

Not the time for this, Ollie thought to himself as he reprimanded himself for lusting after his admittedly handsome neighbor. As he saw the feline open his lips in a soft gasp however a chill ran down the minotaur's spine. He didn't see Archer through the space and when he did turn the corner his eyes widened in horror as he saw the snow leopard on his knees with the tiger's cock in his mouth, which when it thrusted in and out seemed to grow bigger by the second as it was coated by the rubbery goo that dripped from Archer's maw. To his surprise the rubber had already started to spread over both their bodies like wildfire and vines could be seen growing down into the ground and turning the concrete to rubber beneath it. As the tiger started to lower himself down towards the groin of the mutated snow leopard, whose cock was at least twice as big as the minotaur remembered it, he suddenly felt the presence of someone behind him.

Before Ollie could make a run for it a number of vines wrapped around his body and held him in place, anchoring his hooved feet to the ground like roots as he saw the blank muzzle of the kitsune he had seen in the field enter into his range of vision. Xavier had chased him to the farmstead but lost him in the corn, fortunately the snow leopard had already been seeded and informed him of where they were so he could finish the job. His rubber lips split apart and a thick black tongue slithered around the bull before starting to push inside while tiny vines immediately started to spread over his muzzle. The alien creature had already taken over a significant portion of the town by this point and as he pushed his ovipositor against the tailhole of the minotaur and slathered it with more rubber he was able to enjoy seeding this slab of beefcake.

The cheeks of the minotaur bulged as the tongue inside his maw continued to push in, bringing the alien plant that was housed inside of his body with it in order to spread. While he could just seed the creature and let him be a ticking time bomb like the snow leopard was the alien Xavier wanted far more from this creature and thrusted his hips forward into the rubberized butt of the other man. Ollie let out a loud groan as his insides were spread open by the huge, girthy cock that was able to slide deep into him, the alien rubber assimilating his insides almost immediately to make room for the large tentacle cock and seed that was already shifting in preparation in the rubber kitsune's stomach. Just like the plant had done with Xavier initially the alien creature shuddered in pleasure as he felt the spherical object move down the rubber ovipositor and pop inside the bull while rubber covered his head just like the snow leopard and tiger, who had switched positions with the smaller rubber feline thrusting into the bigger striped one as they seeded each other.

Another vessel for their kind, the alien whispered in the mind of the minotaur as they became connected, Ollie quickly losing his sense of self as vines spread over his body and assimilated the flesh to rubber. Even with the tentacle tongue that had slithered down into his throat and bulged out his neck he could see that something had been put inside his stomach, his hands reflexively pressing against the sphere-like object that stretched out his washboard abs. With each seed that was passed to him more of the alien goo came with it, and as it fed into the minotaur's augmented body his rubber biceps and pectorals swelled with new growth. Even as his thoughts were becoming harder to formulate Ollie couldn't help but admire the new physique, especially his cock as the already impressive member began to lengthen while the sensitive flesh rubberized before it was practically down to his knees.

The alien kitsune couldn't help but chuckle as Ollie became yet another alien just like the two rubber creatures that were having sex next to them, their bodies leaking enough of the glowing green goo that it was starting to cause a puddle on the concrete. It would soon be used to nourish the new plant life that would terraform the planet, all from one seed that crashed into the ground. As the alien continued to push his cock deep into the rubbery minotaur to embed seed after seed that stretched out his thick shaft however he felt a hand press against the back of his neck, and for a brief moment both alien and nexus hybrid occupied the same body before the real Xavier was suddenly pulled back and out of the rubber creature that he used to be.

Xavier let out a gasp as he looked down at himself and saw the familiar lithe body and synthetic fur, the vines on his arms and legs wiggling of their own accord as he looked over to see what had happened. "Sorry to spoil your fun," Yavini said with a smirk as he set Xavier down, who continued to stare at essentially himself continuing to thrust the huge rubber cock he had into the growing minotaur whose stomach had started to distend with all the seeds. "But I do believe that your work here is done, time to move on to the final trial."

The kitsune looked back at himself and saw that he did indeed have an eighth tail, and though this one looked like a normal fox one it was rubber in nature and dripped with bright green goo occasionally, and it moved around he could feel something was inside of it. Perhaps it was some of the alien seeds, though as Xavier looked at the creatures that were created from them he wondered if these were also a hybrid of the rubber dragon and plant fox. As the portal was opened for him though he set his mind on the task at hand, getting ready to get the last tail he needed to fulfill his destiny. Whatever the challenge was at hand Xavier knew he was ready for it as he jumped through to the other side.

Chapter Nine – The Final Trial

This was it, Xavier thought to himself as he found himself on the other side of the portal on what appeared to be some sort of campus, he was ready to go and get his last tail. When he looked down at himself he found that he was wearing clothes once more and as he looked around most others were doing the same with everyone around being an anthro this time. There wasn't a whole lot that he could immediately see that gave him hints on what it could be, and he doubted that he would get another meteor to help him out this time. Perhaps this was supposed to be something a little more low-key, Xavier mused as he began to walk around the campus.

After a few minutes Xavier found out that this wasn't some sort of college but instead it was a research campus as he made his way towards one of the buildings. As he saw one of the signs that was pointing out the various wings along with the branch of science it studied and found them all to be extremely advanced in nature. None of them really jumped out at him as something that prompted him towards someone that needed help, and there wasn't any marked as rubber or botany related sciences. One that he did see though was biochemical and decided that was as good a place to start as any as he shifted direction to go down this new path.

When he got into the building the kitsune had to try and not look around in awe even as found himself incredibly impressed with the architecture within. There was clearly a lot of money behind whatever was going on here, Xavier thought to himself as he moved through the lobby. As he saw others walk around him he didn't see any sort of badges or other means to identify them to any sort of security program. It probably was the reason why no one had even batted an eye at him as he walked around and eventually found himself at the cafeteria.

Xavier thought about attempting to buy some food to blend in but he realized that just like every other realm he didn't have any money to pay for anything and he didn't need it with his augmented physiology. But as he looked at the cupcakes that were on display longingly he heard something that caused his ears to twitch. It was two people that were just getting out of the food line themselves and as they passed by the dessert area that the kitsune had looked at longingly he heard them mention something about wishing that something didn't have to happen. Wish fulfillment was his game, Xavier thought to himself as he turned his attention to the cheetah and lizardman that passed by him, and as they headed towards one of the tables to sit down Xavier snuck one of the cupcakes off of the tray with his tail before he walked over and sat down behind them to eat it while listening in.

"I just don't know Terry," the cheetah said as he picked at his food while Xavier eyed . "I know that we're going to be all fine but do we all need to be transferred to different departments? We've been working together for nearly a decade and we know how each other click, we are a well-oiled machine and they're just going to take it apart."

"You know that when a project dies they don't like keeping the team together," the lizardman replied while he ate. "They don't want you to do exactly what you're doing now, which is linger on the past and what could have been and instead focus on the future. Now I'm really sorry Jonas, but we've got until the end of the day for us to get all our files and personal effects in order."

The lizardman named Terry finished up his meal while the cheetah named Jonas continued to just play around with it. While he wasn't quite sure how he would be able to help with some sort of massive tech project that was probably worth millions of dollars. Nevertheless after eight previous trials Xavier felt like he could sense when fate was bringing him the trial that he needed someone to help overcome and decided to go for broke. He was a nexus hybrid after all and if he was going to follow in the footsteps of creatures like Yavini and Renzyl he would need to start being a little more like them, especially after he got to ride along and experience seeing a creature as dominant as that alien warp his thoughts to essentially be a different person.

"Sounds like you have you've been having a rough go at it," Xavier said as he went over and sat down, taking the cheetah man by surprise. "Sorry, couldn't help but overhear, you are getting fired?"

"Oh, no, nothing like that," Jonas replied as he started to eat. "It's not even the fact that we have our project getting canceled either, it's that after ten years and several successful campaigns they're going to break us up. I mean, we're a dream team, and after today we're all just getting split up!"

The cheetah was clearly agitated by this and Xavier could capitalize on it, but the problem was he didn't see anything rubber or plant related other than being in a biochemical research building. Still… he saw an intense desire there to keep the team together and decided to continue to chat with the cheetah about things as he ate. Jonas seemed more than eager to talk to him and after a few minutes of venting asked if Xavier wanted to come and join him in the party for his team. The kitsune was a bit surprised at the invitation but remembered how at ease he felt around Renzyl and even Yavini when they first met, guessing that he had a bit of that mojo as he followed the cheetah to the elevator.

Jonas pushed the proper button for them and as they waited for the car to get to the intended floor the cheetah continued to talk about the team like he was in love with them. Eventually the two got to their destination and when the doors opened Xavier saw that a lame attempt at a party had been attempted by the group with a few things cut out of what looked like copy paper. There was also some snacks that looked like they had raided the vending machine and laid them all over by empty table. Most of the guys that were there all had a dour expression on their faces as they packed up their desks and most didn't even seem to bat an eye that someone had been brought up to their secure lab.

This must be what it's like to be a nexus creature all the time, Xavier thought to himself as he asked for a tour of the place and promptly got one. "So what exactly what were you guys doing up here anyway?" Xavier asked as they passed by the desk of a hyena who just gave the two of them a sad look before putting away a plant, something the kitsune was sure didn't factor into his trial. "Must be something if they got all these people working on it."

"Oh, nothing crazy," Jonas said as they went to a different room that had a bunch of equipment that was already packed up. "We were tasked with designing performance wear that would be able to read a person's biometric signature, but we couldn't seem to find anything that would work through the thick fur of some creatures. We were making headway but I guess the sponsor pulled out of it, so we just have a bunch of half-finished sportswear that can't be used."

"That's too bad," Xavier said as he tried not to let the excitement of the information he was getting show on his face. "I suppose they locked it all away in some secret vault."

"Heh, this was sportswear, not stealth tech," Jonas said as he motioned for Xavier to follow him to another door that he unlocked and opened for him. "This is the fruit of our labor, go ahead and take something if you want. All of it will probably just get tossed in the dumpster anyway."

Jackpot… Xavier felt a smirk cross his muzzle as he saw the rows of shiny clothing glistening at him. "That's very generous of you, going to take a few pairs for yourself?" Xavier asked, the cheetah just shaking his head. "Why not, I think you would look incredibly sexy in this…"

"No, I would just be reminded…" Xavier could see the gears turning in his head as Jonas trailed off before looking at the kitsune. "What was that?" Capitalizing on the twinge of desire that he saw on the cheetah Xavier leaned in and kissed the cheetah deep, instantly getting a powerful response as the other hand of the kitsune rubbed against the growing tent in his pants until they finally broke. “Oh, I guess I wouldn’t mind trying on a piece or two, if you do it with me.”

Xavier felt his smile increase as this cheetah was like putty in his vines, which would soon be the same for their physical body in the real world as he took a view pieces of the clothing that would fit him while Jonas did the same. When he grabbed the shirt he realized the rubbery material did have a slight stretch to it like spandex, but as he let the power he had gotten from Renzyl soak into the fabric it seeped into it like water on a sponge. This was definitely going to do nicely, the kitsune mused as he glanced over and caught a glimpse of the cheetah already changing his clothes. Since it appeared like this was mostly going to be a tail taken for the rubber dragon, probably to balance out the number of plant-based ones he had, Xavier decided he was going to freely indulge in it as he allowed the shiny black material to melt over his own body.

Even though Xavier would have liked to see the reaction on seeing a rubber kitsune approach he decided to take it slow, instead morphing the synthetic material around him so it looked like he was wearing almost a bodysuit with his feet, hands, and head still sticking out of it. When he looked back over at Jonas he had already put on a t-shirt and was struggling a bit with what looked like a pair of rubber briefs or a speedo. The lust and desire that intensified with each tail he had gotten started to manifest inside of him once more and the kitsune decided that he had waited long enough. Xavier walked over just as Jonas managed to get the rubber around his midsection and wrapped his arms around the skinny chest of the other man.

Jonas let out a soft gasp as he felt the bigger man press up against him with the latex on Xavier rubbing against his. It looked like he was about to say something but the kitsune just put a finger to his lips and gave him a lustful smile. Though the feline seemed hesitant at first a quick slide and squeeze of the vulpine hand against his growing bulge in the latex caused the cheetah to practically melt in his embrace. Even without his senses it was clear to Xavier that this creature was quite submissive, and with his ability to see desires he could see a growing appreciation for rubber that was going to serve him just fine.

As the cheetah continued to get petted and groped all along his partially covered body Xavier decided to get started on his trial, which if the feline's desire to be a part of a team really was as strong as he saw was going to make this an interesting one. The kitsune allowed his own encased member to slide free, his rubber cock immediately stiffing as the head instinctively seemed to push against the rubber briefs the cheetah wore. A small grin formed on his face as he wondered if Jonas was thinking it strange that he didn't pull them down yet as he began to press more insistently into his tailhole with the rubber pushing inside of him. He could see the researcher's curiosity starting to get the best of him but Xavier decided to not let him ruin the moment and gently pressed a hand against the feline muzzle of the other man.

The huffs of Jonas soon turned to muffled grunts of surprise as he realized a layer of latex has completely coated his muzzle and left it completely sealed. Xavier's cock was already starting to slide into him and he could feel the rubber shifting in order to spread, infused with the power of the rubber nexus lord dragon. With the kitsune being a bit bigger he used his augmented strength to wrap an arm around the cheetah and lifted him up, feeling his feet kick slightly when they left the ground which only served to wiggle the cock inside him even deeper. With nowhere to go and Xavier shedding the ruse of this being a normal rubbery tryst in the storage closet the kitsune got to work, starting first with the feline bulge that he had continued to knead against.

As Jonas could feel the rubber cock sliding into him it seemed to the feline that it was continuing to get thicker, but what really caught his attention was what was happening to his own groin. He stared down in shock and his breath came out of his nose in huffs as his cock seemed to shrink, melting into the rubber with each push that the kitsune gave to it. The toes of the cheetah curled as the briefs and t-shirt he wore started to spread over his fur, feeling the back of it stick to the kitsune who continued to slowly spread open his insides. While he was both confused and aroused all he could do was let out muffled grunts from the pleasure that came from Xavier continuing to push his cock back into his body.

It didn't take long for Xavier to completely smooth out the groin of the cheetah, feeling the feline wiggle against him as the rubber of the shirt and briefs merged together to form one solid piece. As inch after inch of the kitsune's thickening cock continued to disappear inside of the other male another bulge began to form on the cheetah, the feline's hands pressing against it as the shaft was also lengthening to go deeper inside of him as well. As Jonas attempted to squirm while being hilted though he found it increasingly hard to move his back and when he tried to reach back and use the kitsune's shiny sides to brace himself he let out a muffled gasp as they sank right in! Had the cheetah been able to look back he would have seen that he wasn't the only one that was changing, Xavier's muzzle warping and morphing into something more draconic in appearance as the rubber quickly cascaded over his head.

The rubber on the researcher's face had also started to spread and the blunt feline mouth stretched outwards as though someone was pushing against it from the inside. As it did Jonas found himself able to move his jaws more, but as he stretched them out the rubber went with it and suctioned into his mouth. By this point Xavier had already almost completely assimilated the insides of the cheetah to the point he was more rubber creature than not as he pressed the butt of the feline against his crotch. As the kitsune watched his cock begin to stretch out the stomach of the other male even more he could start to feel their latex-infused flesh fuse together and watched with a bemused grin on his new muzzle as he used his lengthening neck to watch the cheetah's body sink inside of him.

Jonas attempted to remove his hands from the sides of the mutating kitsune but as his arms were pulled into the other rubber body as well the only thing he could focus on was the thick cock that had started to distend his stomach. It was like there was nothing between his body and the throbbing appendage inside him, and the more it stretched him out the more intense the pleasure came to his body. When the rubber of his growing maw finally stretched down into his throat the first thing he did was let out a loud moan as the synthetic skin of his belly seemed to suction around the shaft that now stuck several inches out of him. When Xavier took his own arm, which was no longer needed to prop up the cheetah as the feet of the feline had pressed against his thighs and were immediately pulled in, he stroked his ridged appendage and he could feel the surge of pleasure course through Jonas as his rubberized body mass flowed into him.

Soon the only thing that remained of the researcher was his transforming head, and as a set of horns began to push out of the former cheetah's skull the last of his feline aspects quickly disappeared under the thick black latex that covered him. Both Xavier and Jonas let out similar moans as their necks shifted on their rubber shoulders, which had grown in order to have both of them sit. Soon the rubber hybrid had to turn his head in order to see where the other one had went and as he did so he found a pair of golden eyes staring back at him. For a few brief seconds there was a strange sense of connection and as they blinked at the same time Xavier had trouble remembering which head was his as the last aspects of their heads were finished up.

"X-xavier?" The head on the left asked as he looked down at their shared body, looking back to see the eight rubberized tails of the creature swirling around behind him.

"Yes Jonas?" Xavier replied, his grasp on his identity far stronger than the cheetah. Though the two looked identical he seemed to instinctively be able to know which head he was even when his perspective shifted to the other one when Jonas talked.

"That was… amazing…" Jonas replied as Xavier suddenly felt the hands that had been stroking their cock, which began to soften as it settled down lower until it hung between their legs once again, and felt the fingers press against their thick pectorals. "How did this happen? Did you merge us?"

"Well… that's quite the long story actually," Xavier said as a sheepish grin appeared on his muzzle while the one that used to be the cheetah gave him a slight frown at being denied satisfaction to his curiosity. "I would suggest that you look at this like a gift; I mean, it's going to be impossible to separate your team if your team is all one rubber hydra creature, right?"

It took a second for Jonas to catch on and Xavier couldn't help but grin as he saw a wide smile appear on the other head of the hydra. That was one head on board, Xavier thought to himself as he could feel both happiness and arousal coming from his other side, but that still meant that he had to get the other seven as well. After taking a few minutes the two-headed rubber creature quickly learned how to move their shared body, finding that as long as their thoughts seemed to synchronize with one another their movements were just as fluid and dynamic as if they were one person. The only time they seemed to stumble was if they both wanted to go an opposite direction but they had to actively will for that to happen, and at the moment they both were agreed on what they wanted to do next.

Meanwhile those that were in the office party took notice of the cheetah's leave along with the person they brought along with them after lunch, and after some speculated that he might be curled up in a corner of the lab crying they sent out two people to investigate. Since Vince, a horse man that was their lead data operations manager, and Ronnie, an otter that handled all their sample testing, had already finished up their packing and was just waiting for the others so everyone could go to the bar they volunteered to go look. As they left the main lab and went out to look for their co-worker they both continued to gripe with one another the fact that they were all being reassigned. It was something the entire group had been doing since they got the news and though Jonas was taking it the hardest there was no one in the lab that was happy with the decision.

When the two didn't find them in their storage room or in the sample testing area they decided to move to the break room, which was a small room with a couch for them to crash on along with an old television and a mostly empty vending machine along with a tiny kitchen. They expected that they would find the cheetah curled up on the couch and when they opened the door to look inside they did find someone sitting there, but it wasn't anyone they were expecting. As the muscular rubber creature sat on the piece of furniture one head continued to look at the television screen while the other turned to look at them with a smile on his face. The two were so shocked that they weren't sure what to do and with their brains frozen the only thing they could was stand there and stare at the alien creature whose hand slowly stroked up and down his cock.

"Ah, I thought it might be you two that went looking for me," one of the heads of the hydra said as the creature got up, the other one that had been watching the screen turning to look at them as well. "You know the kitsune I brought up here, right? Well he has given me a way to keep the team together, all we have to do is join up in one body and we can stay one big group!"

"Holy cow… is that you Jonas?" Vince said as the hydra eagerly nodded both heads, causing them to step closer in curiosity. "But… how?"

"That's a long story," the other head said. "One that can be easily told if you join in the fun as your cohort has said."

Though the two were extremely interested in what had happened to their cheetah friend Xavier could sense the hesitation in both of them, especially the horse man as he could see that the otter already had started to adjust the bulge in his khakis. "Jonas, you want us all to just… share a body?" Vince asked. "I know we work great as a team but I'm not sure how all of us in one form is going to help our productivity."

"As you can see our body would come with some great benefits," Jonas said as he flexed his latex muscles, both heads watching

Ronnie practically start to drool. “And while we may be limited to one form it would come with augmented strength and speed that would only compound with more of us together. But that’s nothing compared to our mental bond… imagine sharing data with one another in the blink of an eye, knowing what everyone else was finding out while still being able to work on your own side of the project.”

Xavier had allowed Jonas to make the pitch to his co-workers and the fact that they worked together for so long was starting to show as he could see the face of the equine shift with new emotions. “You… definitely have a point there,” Vince said as Ronnie nodded enthusiastically. “How would we even, you know, join in though, do we need to do something?”

“Well… we could just hug it out until the conversion is complete,” Jonas said as he stepped forward and slid a rubber hand into the waistband, curling the fingers around the stiffening member inside as the equine trembled at the touch. “Or we could have a little more fun with it, like when we hooked up at the Christmas party a few years back.”

It was clear that the two were no strangers to sex and as Ronnie chimed in and said that was fine with him Xavier gathered there was more than one interoffice relationship going on in this place. Having that connection of desire there made it even easier to manipulate the other two as Jonas instructed Vince to have a seat on the couch after getting naked. Even with the mass of two creatures combined the horse was almost as big as them and when he pulled down his pants it revealed a nearly ten-inch-long cock that bounced up and down in the air. After the equine sat down the rubber hydra took his position, the prehensile tails wrapping around and stroking against the somewhat chubby but still fit body of the other male while positioning his tailhole over the throbbing member.

As Jonas and Xavier took their position Ronnie had already gotten naked and was practically stroking himself as he watched the muscular male start to slide down on the thick shaft. Both heads of the hydra let out a groan as the thick cock easily opened their rubberized ring of muscle, their altered anatomy allowing to slide down several inches at once. The sensation of so much of his sensitive flesh being engulfed all at once caused the equine to buck his hips upwards, which only pushed more of his cock inside of them. Both heads huffed and groaned as the hydra quickly worked himself down to the hilt, eager to start the process as the rubber started to spread down the shaft of the horse even before they got to the bottom of it.

Once the rubber hydra sat himself completely on the lap of the horse and was fully impaled by the impressive spire of throbbing flesh Jonas motioned with one of his heads for Ronnie to come over. They could already feel themselves starting to sink down over the body of the horse, the rubber spreading as they pressed their back against the Vince's chest while the otter took position. The couch underneath them creaked in protest with the added weight of a third male as Ronnie lifted his tail and pressed his pucker against the head of their cock. With one shaft already inside of them the sensations were causing both heads to become almost dizzy with lust as they saw the rubber immediately spread over the hole their tip pressed against to make him ready for such an insertion.

"Ohhh… I feel it…" Vince moaned as the lines between their bodies disappeared, the rubber spreading quickly down his sides and over his thighs as the hydra wrapped their large latex feet around his hooves. "It's… so good… like I'm being dipped into a heated pool. I am so deep inside you…"

If the horse was going to say more it was lost by the deep moan as the hydra squeezed around his shaft, though their body was already so pressed against the equine that the head of his cock was clearly outlined right underneath their own. At first they were going to assimilate it with the rest of him but as the hydra watched the otter's increasingly rubbery rear sink down on their shaft an idea came to them. The much smaller male was already being stretched quite a bit from the rubber creature's maleness but Vince let out a loud snort and Ronnie practically squealed as the tip of a second one began to push up into his stretched tailhole as well. Had the rubber not already caused coated the insides of the otter it would have been impossible to do but as the body of the horse disappeared into the hydra his shaft double penetrated the other male and caused his furry stomach to stretch out even more lewdly. As the hands of the horse stroked their muscular chest Xavier could feel his shoulders starting to pull in, the rubber defying gravity to rise up Vince's already elongating neck, but instead of sinking into his pectorals that they were massaging the rubber merely coated them.

Most of Vince's body was indistinguishable from the hydra as the rubber creature continued to sink down into him, but as their increasingly shared body rippled and warped he felt his arms start to swell instead of be assimilated. With his new neck he was able to watch as the mass from the rest of his body seemed to get pumped into them, the muscle thickening underneath the rubber skin as it rippled all the way down his forearms and to his hands. Soon his fingers were morphing into a copy of those that were above it and as thick rubbery claws grew from them Jonas and Xavier flexed them along with their first set. That would certainly help with their physical efficiency, Xavier thought to himself as the equine muzzle pushing up next to him was stretched open while rubber covered and mutated it to look like his own, especially when he found himself able to dictate control over one hand while the other two could manipulate the others.

Unlike the equine though there would be nothing of the much smaller otter that they would keep on their shared body as the hydra gripped the rubberized sides to keep pushing him down. Already the thick tail of the other man had been absorbed into the stomach of the now three-headed creature as Vince's head sprouted a pair of horns from the last of the rubber covering it. Their combined cocks and growing physique had rendered the otter little more than a cock sheath and they decided that they would speed the process along. As one pair of hands continued to push him down so they could thrust deep and assimilate his insides the other pair pressed the body of the otter man down on their expanding form. By this point Ronnie's head was practically nestled between their mountainous pectorals and as soon as the rubber touched fur he began to sink inside.

The rubber spread briefly over the otter's face but as the hydra humped up into him his body was quickly assimilated. The three heads watched as the look of extreme pleasure became frozen on Ronnie's muzzle before it disappeared into the chest of the creature along with the rest of him, eventually their two cocks flopping back out when the last of the mass was absorbed into their forms. For a brief moment they wondered if they hadn't done something bad by accident but it wasn't long before they felt their shoulders and chest of their hulking form shift and a large bulge rise up on one of them. The three heads smiled at one another as they saw a forth rubber hydra head quickly emerge, a loud and deep moan reverberating through his stretching neck as it reformed and joined the cluster that was already there.

With the other two assimilated the four-headed creature realized that while they had gained more consciousnesses that shared one body they actually were able to control their huge four-armed form even more. Things like refined movements became incredibly easy when there were more than two perspectives working in perfect harmony as they got up from the couch that had collapsed from their lustful merging. Jonas chattered happily with Vince and Ronnie and though they all had the same voice Xavier could see their personalities shining through with each head even though they were all synchronized. After a few moments where the two newly converted creatures got used to their new tails and all four figured out their two sets of limbs they smiled at once as they realized that it had been a while since they had rejoined the party…

Much to Xavier's surprise the introduction of a four-headed rubber hydra hulk to the rest of the team went over surprisingly well, and in less than an hour not only were they a nine-headed beast of a creature with a massive set of legs and two sets of arms but also a pair of wings that could act as a third set of arms as necessary. They also had decided that two cocks were not enough and as they began to move their desks around in order to maximize efficiency he could see that one set of hands had started to stroke the four identical rubber members that were nestled between their huge shiny thighs. While he was sad to leave the group Xavier had decided to give them some time to themselves, especially when the lizardman that was their group supervisor came in and they practically pounced on him to absorb him into the fold as their true nineth head, after they had gotten what he wanted. As he looked back at the rubber tail he had gained he watched it as the tip split into eight more separate smaller rubber tendrils that were still attached at the base.

"It seems that you really have a way of bringing people together," Renzyl said, Xavier turning around to see that both him and Yavini were suddenly standing there behind him.

"They were the ones that wanted to be that way," Xavier replied with a grin as he watched the hydra get to work at an intense pace. "I just helped facilitate things."

"Now that is quite an answer," Yavini stated. "You're going to do quite well as a nexus hybrid, especially now that your trial is at an end. Tell me, was it everything that you didn't know you hoped for when we first met?"

Xavier looked back at his tails, all of them back to their original states, and as he looked over each of them he remembered those he met in order to get it. "Yeah, I think it was," Xavier said with a smile on his muzzle before he turned his attention back to the two nexus creatures. "So what do I do now, continue to go out and help people with their problems? Or is there something else that my new Lords wish of me?"

"I see that someone has definitely gotten into the role," Renzyl replied with a chuckle as he put an arm around the shoulder of the kitsune. "You can go and do what you like, that's the perk of being a nexus beast is the autonomy you have from the rest of our realm. However Yavini mentioned something to me and we've been working on a little gift that I think you might enjoy..."

Chapter Ten – End of a Journey

As the sun went down on the forest the wolf that was within it let out a soft sigh as he looked down at his trail map. All Alister wanted to do was try out the new trail that he had found when he went into the park and didn't expect it to be an all-day encounter. At first he thought that he had just misinterpreted the new loop but while he was still on some sort of man-made path it was slowly dawning on him that he was likely no longer on anything the map showed anymore. Part of him wanted to try and circle back but that would mean that he would be spending nearly the entirety of the night picking his way through the darkness. When he got to the base of a somewhat large hill he had also found stones that looked like stairs situated next to a river and hoped that this was a sign that he had made the loop and was on his way back towards civilization.

Alister silently prayed that he wasn't going to find himself further out in the woods and that he would need some sort of rescue squad as he slowly made his way up, his already tired legs straining as he climbed the rather impressive set of stairs that led upwards. Though the path was relatively straight-forward it had twists and turns, soon he had found himself losing where he had started as the base of the hill disappeared amongst the trees. The river was still there though and he could tell as the rushing water grew more intense that he had to be getting close to the source of it as he panted loudly. Just when he thought that his body couldn't take any more the land evened out and the lupine's eyes widened in surprise when he found himself standing in front of a large, ornate wooden door set into a wall that cut through the forest itself.

It was something he definitely didn't expect to find as the wolf looked at the intricate engraving of a nine-tailed fox in what appeared to be a meditative pose. As he looked to the side he could see that the river was beyond the wall as the water rushed out of an opening underneath it. Since he had no intention of trying to swim inside Alister grabbed onto the shiny bronze handle and gave it a tug, which to his surprise nearly caused him to stumble back as the rounded door swung open easily. The wolf cautiously stepped forward before he looked on the other side of the wall and what he saw was even more surprising than finding a wall with a door in it on top of a hill in the middle of the forest.

Almost immediately the wolf felt like he had entered into some sort of courtyard or monastery as he saw a polished, shiny fountain in the middle of a cobblestone pathway. As he passed through the door he turned when he heard it close behind him and saw two similarly shiny statues that like the fountain were all shaped in the image of a kitsune. Was this some sort of fox temple, Alister thought to himself, and as he slowly moved in further he saw that he was not alone. A small group of vulpines came out of one of the buildings and as they walked along the courtyard he could see that all of them had more than one tail attached to him. As he stood there gawking at them he saw one of them turn and see him, which prompted the others to do so as well.

"Um, hi there," Alister said as he went up to the group, noting they all wore bright green robes that shimmered in the light. "I think I may have gotten a bit lost and wound up in your… uh, what is this place exactly?"

"This is the Court of the Nine Tails," the one with four tails, which was the most out of any of them, said as he stepped forward. "Here we help those who need it in exchange for earning our tails, which much like karma itself follows us everywhere. If you have come to this place then you are not lost, I thought the same way myself when I arrived at that door and now I couldn't be happier."

Cult alert, Alister thought to himself as the others nodded. "Right… well, I just need to find the path to get back to the parking lot," Alister said. "If you can just point me in the right direction I'll just be on my way."

"I'm afraid that might not be such a good idea," another voice chimed in, both Alister and the kitsune turning to see a dark green and white furred kitsune wearing a red outfit was suddenly next to him with a smile on his muzzle. "The hill provides a deceitful view of time, even if you start back down now it's going to be very dark and your parking lot is ages away. Fortunately for you we have plenty of space to accommodate, even though we've had quite a bit of growth lately we have a lot of room left to spare."

Alister believed this kitsune in particular to be the leader from the way the others looked on in awe at him, and the wolf found himself strangely at ease and nodded his head, then followed him away from the group and towards a different building. "My name is Alister," the wolf introduced. "Like I was telling the others I was just hiking around and stumbled upon this place."

"Well as I'm sure they told you no one quite stumbles upon here," the kitsune replied with a soft chuckle as Alister felt one of the tails brush up against him. "My name is Xavier, and in the briefest of explanations this is my domain. You must be extremely tired though, I know from personal experience that the hike to this place can be quite strenuous and we're dedicated to taking care of people."

Alister just nodded and as Xavier tilted his head away in order to allow himself a little smirk. Ever since he had once more emerged from the pool that had started this entire journey and found himself back at a rejuvenated temple he had been gaining more followers. All of them seemed to have the same story of hiking and getting lost in the hills while following a trail, and most of them stuck around after he showed them a nexus hybrid's brand of hospitality. Even before they got started the kitsune could sense that wolf wasn't going to take much as he brought him to a place where half a dozen foxes were eating.

Xavier told Alister to feel free to have whatever he would like and though the wolf tried to say he wasn't hungry his stomach had an ill-timed and very loud gurgle that caused him to grin sheepishly. The kitsune used one of his tails to motion the lupine to the chow line before heading to one of the empty tables to await him. It was only a few minutes before Alister returned with a rather large plate of food that came from what seemed like all manner of different kinds that were there. It was only natural, Alister thought, as the catering had come from Lord Jerkah as a gift for being a steward to this extra-dimensional space and to help with new converts.

"This is the best thing I think I've ever had," Alister commented after swallowing down a mouthful of steak. "I thought that it'd be some sort of vegetarian spread or something like that."

"We find that its best to have very few rules in order to compliment a variety of tastes, and not just dietary," Xavier explained as he watched the wolf continue to eat. "Basically as long as you want to help people you are welcome here… though a fondness for foxes doesn't hurt. That being said once you are done eating I'll show you around, though I imagine once you are done eating you will be quite tired."

Though Alister was about to say that the food was helping the wolf heard a strange hiss that seemed to come out of nowhere that broke his line of thought. When he remembered it again he did notice that the activity of the day was bearing down on him, something that he relayed to the kitsune who merely nodded his head. Once he was finished he was told to leave his tray there and to follow Xavier to another part of the courtyard, which he found himself doing as they went back outside. The wolf was surprised to see that night had already fallen and was actually glad that the kitsune hadn't let him go back down the mountain as they moved to one of the larger units that was covered in vines with purple flowers.

As Alister was shown inside however he felt something that once more caused him embarrassment, though this time it was related something a little lower than his stomach. Fortunately the kitsune was walking slightly ahead of him as he started to grow erect, his shaft twitching within the confines of his pants as he tried to adjust himself. He wasn't sure why this had suddenly happened but he couldn't stop himself and was getting harder by the second as he let out a small whine. If he had any sort of magical sight he would have seen what Xavier saw, which was his ethereal blue tail pushing into his groin to cause it to get aroused for him.

“So this is my personal room,” Xavier said as he turned around, which caused the wolf to turn and try and hide himself. “Oh… it appears that you have more needs than just hunger. Perhaps I can help satisfy that one as well.”

“Oh no, it’s fine!” Alister quickly said as he attempted to right back out the door. “I think I’ll just sleep outside!”

The wolf let out a gasp as he suddenly found his arm getting pulled back by something strong, and at first Alister thought that the kitsune had closed the distance between them and grabbed his wrist. When he looked down though his jaw dropped as he saw what looked like a green vine had looped around him and as he was pulled back he could feel it coil up underneath his shirt. “Oh god, it’s an alien cult!” Alister shouted as he tried to stop himself only to continue to be slowly slid across the floor back towards Xavier. “I promise if you let me go I won’t tell anyone, just don’t eat my brain.”

“Oh, you’re one of those,” Xavier replied as he rolled his eyes and let the robe he was wearing fall to the floor, which only caused the wolf to freeze as he saw that the tails behind the kitsune were not only all different but were wiggling and moving in ways that should have been impossible. “Although I suppose you’re not too far off, especially with the alien thing, but I promise not to eat your brains or anything like that. Now given the fact that you’re still hard as a rock despite thinking that I assume that you find my form at least aesthetically pleasing?”

The calm voice of the kitsune as well as the assurances that he wouldn’t be attacked seemed to be enough to at least calm down Alister enough to keep him from fighting back or raving about aliens. “I… I suppose you are,” Alister replied as he looked the now naked man up and down. “But… your tails…”

"My tails are not important at the moment," Xavier replied as he continued to wave the others around, keeping the wolf spellbound while he talked. While he could have just used his snake tail to try and enthrall him, which he already did a little while it was disguised, it required a lighter trance to do what he was about to. "What's important is you, and the choice that you are about to make."

"I am?" Alister asked in confusion.

"Indeed you are," Xavier replied. "It's not even going to be that hard of one, all I'm asking is that you trust me enough to let my tails do what they do best in order to get you into a more comfortable state while engaging in more… lustful acts. If you allow me to do that then we can start opening your mind to the possibilities of this place, but if you really think that I'm some sort of alien cult leader than I'll send you on your way and even get you back to your car in the parking lot without you needing to take another single step."

Xavier turned away and allowed Alister to think about the offer he had just gave him, not wanting to influence it at all as he went to an area of his room and laid against one of the large pillows there. While it wasn't uncommon for one of his acolytes to be there with him, especially if they were getting close to becoming full kitsunes that would likely join either Renzyl or, more likely, Yavini, he made sure the chambers were empty so that he could have the wolf all to himself. Xavier used one of his tails to grab a bundle of grapes to feed himself with while he waited but didn't even get to the second one before he saw the wolf enter into his field of vision. It was clear that he had made his choice since it triggered one of the small hypnotic commands that rendered the lupine naked in front of him.

"You made a good choice," Xavier said as he stood up with a grin on his face. "Now that you're trusting me it's time I make good on my promise."

The wolf let out a slight yelp as he suddenly found himself lifted up into the air while something once more coiled around his body, though this time it was not only around his wrists but also his ankles and around his waist and neck as well. When he looked at himself he saw that there were shiny black tentacles that had wrapped around him and when he traced them back to the kitsune he was shocked to find that they seemed to all technically come from only one of his tails. Though he squirmed slightly in the grasp of the surprisingly strong appendages as they squeezed around his muscles it was rather rhythmic in nature and felt a bit like a massage as Xavier walked up and traced a finger down his still hard cock.

Xavier wasn't even close to being done with the wolf yet though and took his pool toy tail and pressed it up against the lupine's face. The kitsune could hear muffled noises coming from the other man as he tried to talk with a face full of rubber but it wasn't long before it pressed inside his muzzle and effectively gagged him while also introducing spores that the air inside was laced with. That combined with the passive hypnosis helped put the wolf in a relaxed state as he felt the muscles of the lupine start to slacken in his grasp. As the pool toy tail continued to keep itself adhered to his muzzle, which had begun to distort under the rubber, Xavier took an entirely different tail and snaked it up between the wolf's legs.

As Alister started to feel his mind buzzing while being suspended in the air, the kitsune still teasing his cock, his body suddenly jolted in pleasure as something else began to push up inside of him. Xavier slowly eased in his gooey tapered dragon tail as he waited for the conversion process to start, rubberizing his insides to allow his seed tail to push up into him. The wolf let out a loud groan as he was penetrated and as more of the rubbery appendage disappeared inside of him, the goo spreading over his rear end. He could feel Alister quivering in his grip at the pleasure of being filled and once he was finished with making sure his insides could take what was next he pulled the semi-solid tail out and switched it with his seed tail instead.

Unlike before though he was only going to put one very specific seed inside of this one as he used his rubber and vine tails to stroke against the cock of the wolf to keep him stimulated. Alister let out a muffled groan into the rubber that surrounded his muzzle as something else spread open his tailhole, bumping against his prostate before going even deeper. Though he didn't know that he had already been converted on the inside he could tell that something even stranger was going on as he felt a bump of something spherical against his tailhole. At first he thought the kitsune had used his own cock to thrust into him but when he was able to look down he saw Xavier standing there with a pleasured look on his face and stroking his own cock as something large and round pushed up into him through the tail.

The insertion caused Alister to orgasm almost instantly, especially as the other two tails had gotten into a rhythm to stroke the thickening cock as rubber covered the sensitive flesh. His grey fur was assimilated by the black substance as he continued to writhe in the air and thrust his hips, though as the seed germinated inside of him the shiny material turned to a bright red as it covered over his chest and back. Even though the transforming wolf could feel the changes in his body the only thing he could do was wiggle his body in pleasure, and when the pool toy tail pulled away from his face he was able to let out a loud moan. When he inhaled again though he suddenly found his angular vulpine muzzle filled with silver fox tail, which as soon as he did he let out a grunt as his thin body immediately began to swell with new muscle all over his growing physique.

Xavier couldn't help but admire his newest creation as the fox's groans grew slightly deeper from the moonbloom pollen in the silver tail. Even though he had already orgasmed once the former wolf's maleness had started to harden again, but instead of continuing to get stroked by the other tails he found his growing paws press against the ground. "Ohhh… uggghhh…" Alister said as he looked at his hands and watched his fingernails turn to claws while his flat chest and stomach popped with new pectorals and abs underneath spreading synthetic latex skin. "What's… going… on…"

"I told you I was going to make you more comfortable around here," Xavier replied with a grin as he watched the confused rubber muscle fox look at his new thick arms covered in the shiny material. "What better way to do that then to be a fox yourself? Admittedly you were the first that I used most of my tails on at once and I'm wondering if that was a little overboard, but while you wait for all the spores inside you to wear off why don't you put that cock of yours to good use as my way of helping you relax."

Though Alister could still think it was like his thoughts were walking through mud as Xavier went back to the pillows and used his tails to indicate where the lust and spore addled fox should go, which caused the muscular rubber creature's face to light up. As the kitsune felt the new rubber fox press against him it was at least clear that any reservations he had about being here were no longer a thing, especially when he felt the head of his throbbing tool start to push inside of him. As the clawed hands pressed against his hips for better leverage it reminded Xavier of his first tail and caused him to smile, especially knowing that the werewolf out there had turned his entire tribe into similar creatures that prowled with him in the woods below when their dimensions linked up.

Xavier had actually been allowed to visit all of the places that he had helped before he got his first convert, who had arrived about a day after he set up shop looking for enlightenment and ended up with the two of them having rather passionate sex. From the werewolf tribe he had gone to the planet of ghosts where he saw that Nautlin was thriving and was even powerful enough to transform the kitsune into an aquatic shark creature again where the two of them could rut while under the water. From there it was the city, though he didn't stay there long when he saw that vines had grown over the majority of buildings and that most of the people there were walking vine monsters. He also visited the goo dragons, the rubber hydra, the pool toys, and even the farmstead that had been completely terraformed into an alien landscape, the latter of which he also quickly left to make sure he didn't get caught up in their particular transformation again.

A particularly hard thrust from the creature behind him brought Xavier back to the present along with the surge of pleasure that came with it, and as he looked back at Alister he could see that the former wolf was definitely much more comfortable. As his own body was pushed down into the pillow from the rutting male on top of him the kitsune used his tails to stimulate the big fox further. Once Alister had a chance to sate his newfound desires and the spores cleared his system, which would still leave him as a lithe rubber fox, he could talk to him on whether he wished to keep his new body and try to earn tails like him or if he wanted to go back.

As Xavier's body rocked back and forth from the force of the cock sliding in and out of him the smiling kitsune had an inkling he, like many of the others in his position before him, was probably going to accept their own nine-tail trial.

Made in the USA
Columbia, SC
03 February 2022